You're About to Become a

Privileged

Woman.

INTRODUCING
PAGES & PRIVILEGES™.

It's our way of thanking you for buying
our books at your favorite retail store.

— *GET ALL THIS FREE* —
WITH JUST ONE PROOF OF PURCHASE:

◆ Hotel Discounts up to 60% at home and abroad

◆ Travel Service - Guaranteed lowest published
airfares plus 5% cash back on tickets

◆ $25 Travel Voucher

◆ Sensuous Petite Parfumerie collection ($50 value)

◆ Insider Tips Letter with sneak previews of
upcoming books

◆ Mystery Gift (if you enroll before 6/15/95)

You'll get a FREE personal card, too.
It's your passport to all these benefits– and to
even more great gifts & benefits to come!
There's no club to join. No purchase commitment. No obligation.

As a *Privileged Woman,*
you'll be entitled to all
these *Free Benefits.*
And *Free Gifts,* too.

To thank you for buying our books, we've designed an exclusive FREE program called *PAGES & PRIVILEGES™.* You can enroll with just one Proof of Purchase, and get the kind of luxuries that, until now, you could only read about.

*B*IG HOTEL DISCOUNTS

A privileged woman stays in the finest hotels. And so can you—at up to 60% off! Imagine standing in a hotel check-in line and watching as the guest in front of you pays $150 for the same room that's only costing you $60. Your *Pages & Privileges* discounts are good at Sheraton, Marriott, Best Western, Hyatt and thousands of other fine hotels all over the U.S., Canada and Europe.

*F*REE DISCOUNT TRAVEL SERVICE

A privileged woman is always jetting to romantic places.
When <u>you</u> fly, just make one phone call for the lowest published airfare at time of booking—<u>or double the difference back</u>! PLUS—

you'll get a $25 voucher to use the first time you book a flight AND <u>5% cash back on every ticket you buy thereafter through the travel service</u>!

FREE GIFTS!

A privileged woman is always getting wonderful gifts.
Luxuriate in rich fragrances that will stir your senses (and his). This gift-boxed assortment of fine perfumes includes three popular scents, each in a beautiful designer bottle.   <u>Truly Lace</u>...This luxurious fragrance unveils your sensuous side. <u>L'Effleur</u>...discover the romance of the Victorian era with this soft floral. <u>Muguet des bois</u>...a single note floral of singular beauty. This $50 value is yours—FREE when you enroll in *Pages & Privileges*! And it's just the beginning of the gifts and benefits that will be coming your way!

$50 VALUE

FREE INSIDER TIPS LETTER

A privileged woman is always informed. And you'll be, too, with our free letter full of fascinating information and sneak previews of upcoming books.

MORE GREAT GIFTS & BENEFITS TO COME

A privileged woman always has a lot to look forward to.
And so will you. You get all these wonderful FREE gifts and benefits now with only one purchase...and there are no additional purchases required. However, each additional retail purchase of Harlequin and Silhouette books brings you a step closer to even more great FREE benefits like half-price movie tickets...and even more FREE gifts like these beautiful fragrance gift baskets:

L'Effleur...This basketful of romance lets you discover L'Effleur from head to toe, heart to home.
Truly Lace...A basket spun with the sensuous luxuries of Truly Lace, including Dusting Powder in a reusable satin and lace covered box.

ENROLL NOW!
Complete the Enrollment Form on the back of this card and become a Privileged Woman today!

Enroll Today in *PAGES & PRIVILEGES*™,
the program that gives you Great Gifts
and Benefits with just one purchase!

Enrollment Form

☐ *Yes!* I WANT TO BE A *PRIVILEGED WOMAN*.

Enclosed is one *PAGES & PRIVILEGES*™ Proof of Purchase from
any Harlequin or Silhouette book currently for sale in stores (Proofs of
Purchase are found on the back pages of books) and the store cash register
receipt. Please enroll me in *PAGES & PRIVILEGES*™. Send my Welcome
Kit and FREE Gifts -- and activate my FREE benefits -- immediately.

▶ DETACH HERE AND MAIL TODAY! ▶

NAME (please print)
_____

ADDRESS _____ APT. NO _____

CITY _____ STATE _____ ZIP/POSTAL CODE _____

PROOF OF PURCHASE

SAMPLE ONLY

Please allow 6-8 weeks for delivery. Quantities are
limited. We reserve the right to substitute items.
Enroll before October 31, 1995 and receive
one full year of benefits.

**NO CLUB!
NO COMMITMENT!**
*Just one purchase brings
you great Free Gifts
and Benefits!*
(See inside for details.)

Name of store where this book was purchased_____

Date of purchase_____

Type of store:

    ☐ Bookstore   ☐ Supermarket   ☐ Drugstore

    ☐ Dept. or discount store (e.g. K-Mart or Walmart)

    ☐ Other (specify)_____

Which Harlequin or Silhouette series do you usually read?

_____

Complete and mail with one Proof of Purchase and store receipt to:

U.S.: *PAGES & PRIVILEGES*™, P.O. Box 1960, Danbury, CT 06813-1960

Canada: *PAGES & PRIVILEGES*™, 49-6A The Donway West, P.O. 813,
North York, ON M3C 2E8   **PRINTED IN U.S.A**

She knew she still loved him

"Dirk, I'm sorry," she'd insisted pleadingly. "I'll be my old self again once I conceive. And it's only a matter of time. The doctor said there's nothing wrong with me. He...he says I need to relax and—"

Dirk's bitter laugh cut her off. "Relax, Laura? Making love to you these days is like making love to a spring that's wound so tight I'm almost afraid you'll snap if I touch you. Well, it's me who's snapped, my darling. I've had enough. I'm out of this marriage!"

MIRANDA LEE is Australian, living near Sydney. Born and raised in the Bush, she was boarding-school educated and briefly pursued a classical music career before moving to Sydney and embracing the world of computers. Happily married, with three daughters, she began writing when family commitments kept her at home. She likes to create stories that are believable, modern, fast-paced and sexy. Her interests include reading meaty sagas, doing word puzzles, gambling and going to the movies.

Books by Miranda Lee

HARLEQUIN PRESENTS
1651—A DATE WITH DESTINY
1664—A DARING PROPOSITION
1702—KNIGHT TO THE RESCUE
1728—MARRIAGE IN JEOPARDY

Miranda LEE

AN OUTRAGEOUS PROPOSAL

Harlequin Books

TORONTO • NEW YORK • LONDON
AMSTERDAM • PARIS • SYDNEY • HAMBURG
STOCKHOLM • ATHENS • TOKYO • MILAN
MADRID • WARSAW • BUDAPEST • AUCKLAND

ISBN 0-373-11737-X

AN OUTRAGEOUS PROPOSAL

Copyright © 1992 by Miranda Lee.

First North American Publication 1995.

This edition published by arrangement with Harlequin Enterprises B.V.

® and TM are trademarks of the publisher. Trademarks indicated with
® are registered in the United States Patent and Trademark Office, the
Canadian Trade Marks Office and in other countries.

Printed In U.S.A.

CHAPTER ONE

THE curtain came down at half-time, with Laura clapping as long and loudly as everyone else. Once again, it looked as if Morrie had brought off a directing miracle, creating an exciting and professional-looking musical from a relatively inexperienced group of amateur players. She couldn't imagine even the Broadway version of *South Pacific* gaining any better reaction from its audience than this suburban rendition. The North Sydney Musical Theatre Group and its genius of a director could really take a bow!

Of course, the wonderful and eye-catching costumes had helped, Laura thought, smiling to herself with warm satisfaction as the lights came on and she rose from her seat on the aisle.

The smile didn't last for long, was wiped from her face once she turned and saw who was sitting right behind her. Her teeth clamped down hard in her jaw, her stomach immediately in knots.

Strange . . . She had half expected to see him here tonight. Morrie was, after all, his brother. But the reality of finally confronting her estranged husband again after their last shattering encounter affected Laura much more than she could ever have imagined. Everything inside her seemed to lock tight, as though in defence of the pain that welled up within her.

But along with the pain was a bitter determination not to let *him* see her distress.

'Dirk,' she greeted him with a polite nod.

'Laura,' he returned in that deeply resonant voice which had swayed countless juries over to his point of view.

She fought to keep her blue eyes steady as they met his cool grey ones. Not an easy task at all. Dirk's penetrating and intuitive scrutiny had been the undoing of many a wobbly witness. He never blinked, merely set a steely gaze on his prey till he or she was forced to look away in agitation, thereby betraying a weakness which he then zeroed in on with ruthless resolve.

Before he could claim victory in her case she let her eyes slide nonchalantly across to the voluptuous brunette sitting next to him. Clearly, she was his date, since her arm was wound tightly around his like a boa constrictor.

Well . . . he'd always said he preferred brunettes, Laura conceded caustically, thinking of her own shoulder-length black hair. Though this was where any resemblance between herself and this creature ceased. She wouldn't have been seen dead wearing that much make-up. Or that *dress*, for that matter. Good God, the stupid woman wouldn't want to breathe in too deeply or her breasts would pop right out!

Too late Laura realised she was glaring at the brunette and her possessive hold as though she wanted to tear those scarlet-nailed fingertips from her husband's flesh.

I'm showing my jealousy, she realised with a deep jab of dismay. Forcing a wary smile to her lips, she glanced back at Dirk, who was still watching her closely.

Nothing new in that. Dirk was an inveterate observer of people, priding himself on their rarely being able to fool him. Laura knew she had once again betrayed far too much of her residual feelings for the man, but there didn't seem to be much she could do about it except decamp as quickly as possible.

'Sorry I can't stay and chat,' she went on with a creditable lack of sarcasm. 'I promised Carmel to join her at intermission. I hope you enjoy the rest of the show.'

To her horror, Laura felt tears prick her eyes as she hurried on up the carpeted steps. And to think she had imagined only this last week that she was finally getting over the man! It seemed she still had quite some way to go before she could successfully kill and bury her love for Dirk Thornton.

But believe me, she vowed vehemently to herself, I'm going to work on it!

'Laura! Oh, Laura! Over here...'

Laura just had time to blink the telling moisture from her eyes before being descended upon by Carmel, Morrie's wife, who took her arm and shepherded her out into the foyer, chatting away all the time.

'Isn't the show marvellous so far? I didn't realise Sharon and Bob could sing so well. Not that their singing alone carried the first half. The dancing is fantastic and your costumes were simply stunning. But honestly, Laura, if Morrie weren't such a good dentist and we didn't have two children to bring up, I really think I'd encourage him to try directing theatre for a living. I mean he...'

Laura allowed Carmel's pride in her husband full rein, putting in the occasional murmur of approval where required. But underneath her composed smiling exterior she was still deeply agitated by her response to seeing Dirk with that woman.

'My God, there's Dirk!' Carmel suddenly exclaimed in a shocked tone.

Laura's heart jumped. Gathering herself, she turned her eyes to once again encounter the unwanted vision of her husband and the brunette together, though they were blessedly on the other side of the crowded foyer.

'I knew Morrie sent him tickets,' Carmel whispered harshly, 'but I didn't think he'd have the gall to come—especially not with something like that!'

'Don't concern yourself on my account,' Laura bit out. 'I've already seen her. She and Dirk are sitting right behind me.'

Carmel's eyes spoke volumes as they turned towards her. 'Oh, how awful for you! Would you like me to see if I can find you a seat elsewhere for the second half?'

'Certainly not!' Laura countered sharply. Pride demanded that Dirk think she didn't give a damn where he sat, or with whom.

'Yes, but——'

'No buts, Carmel,' Laura insisted. 'I was bound to run into Dirk sooner or later with one of his women. Better *sooner*, from the way I felt inside when I actually saw him with...with...' She shuddered at the mental image of what Dirk would undoubtedly be doing to the sexy brunette later that evening.

If anyone had told her a year ago that her husband would become a philandering rake, she would not have believed them. But over the past few months evidence of his womanising had filtered down to her through a girl she worked with. The female in question did not like Laura, because Laura had been promoted to buyer over her. Claudia seemed very happy to relay news of the many glamorous women Laura's husband had been squiring around Sydney. It wasn't just speculation, either. Claudia shared a flat with Dirk's secretary—a silly woman who just loved to talk. The gossip had hurt Laura, but not as much as actually seeing her husband in action.

Carmel was staring at her with real sympathy in her face. 'You're still in love with him, aren't you? Oh, you poor darling...'

The woman's gentle pity sent the lump crowding back into Laura's throat, making her voice thick and husky when she spoke. 'Not for much longer, I hope. All I need to do is keep on seeing him with women like that and I...I'll...' She shook her head and let her eyes drop to the floor, no longer able to hide her wretched vulnerability.

'It's a pity,' Carmel sympathised, 'that Dirk's so damned attractive. It must be hard to forget a man like that, let alone find someone else to measure up.'

Laura found her eyes lifting to stare across at the man she'd married nearly four years ago. He was dressed in an elegant dark suit, and there was no denying he was the sort of man who would always stand out in a crowd. But it was more than just a combination of a tall, well-proportioned body, a strongly handsome face and a thatch of thick silvery blond hair. He had a presence, an aura, that commanded attention wherever he went.

Perhaps it was a product of the profession he was in. Perhaps he'd cultivated that commanding air of authority to impress juries and undermine opposing lawyers. Perhaps... But somehow Laura had the feeling Dirk had grown up with it already built-in.

Her stomach curled at the way his companion was fawning all on him.

'He *looks* the same,' she said sharply. 'But he's not. He's changed.'

'Yes... He certainly has. All that running around with fast flashy women! It's funny, though,' Carmel went on, a puzzled frown marring her pretty face. 'Whenever he drops in to see Morrie and the kids, he's just like the old Dirk we used to know and love. It's only when I try to talk to him about why he left a lovely girl like you for a life of empty women-chasing that he changes. Tells me to mind my own damned business then dashes off to meet some new woman or other. Not that he brings any of his hussies to *our* place. I wouldn't stand for it. I told him that the only woman of his that was welcome in *my* home was his wife!'

Laura looked at Carmel with a mixture of affection and guilt. Much as she didn't condone Dirk's behaviour these days, there *were* extenuating circumstances over the actual break-up of their marriage. But if she started explaining them, other facts would come out, facts which Dirk had demanded she keep secret.

'You shouldn't be worrying about *my* feelings, Carmel,' she urged. 'Once Dirk gets round to legalising our separation with a divorce, I'll be his ex-wife and we won't even be related any more. Dirk is Morrie's brother, and Donna's and Nicholas's uncle. Don't sour your relationship with him on account of me. *Please.*'

Carmel shook her head in frustration. 'I don't know how you can be so generous after the way he's treated you. But what has our being related got to do with our friendship? I mean...we *are* still friends, aren't we, Laura? You know, I've really missed you coming round, and so have the children. Aren't Morrie and I ever going to see you again outside of this theatre group?'

Laura's smile was slightly cracked around the edges. 'Well, I *was* going to come to your party tonight after the show...'

Carmel grabbed both her hands, pressing them quite vigorously. 'Oh, but you must still come. Dirk won't be there with that woman, I can assure you. He wouldn't dare!'

Laura laughed, and at that moment she met Dirk's eyes across the room. Her insides tightened, but she refused to look away. She held his gaze without flinching and was literally floored when he suddenly smiled at her.

It was not the sort of sardonic smile she might have expected, but a very knowing, sexy smile designed to flatter its female recipient, to make her feel extremely feminine and desirable. Now Laura *did* look away, appalled by the very real heat that began to creep up her neck and into her cheeks.

The expression 'Saved by the bell' took on a literal meaning when the buzzer heralded that the second half of the show would shortly begin. Laura was only too willing to scuttle back into the darkening theatre and huddle in her seat, her eyes fixed staunchly on the stage ahead.

But nothing could stop her knowing the very second the couple behind took their seats. Damn, but she could feel Dirk's mocking eyes upon the back of her head, could almost see him smiling in satisfaction at how easily he'd brought that blush to her face.

A deep frown scrunched up her brow as she thought about how stirred she'd felt when he'd smiled at her. It had been a long time since Dirk had affected her like that with a mere glance. A long, long time.

Her eyes squeezed tightly shut against the old rush of guilt that consumed her every time she thought of what her obsession over having a baby had done to their relationship, particularly their sex life. Towards the end, she hadn't let Dirk make love to her unless she could possibly conceive. Even then, he hadn't been able to arouse her, her mind being on nothing else but whether a child would result from the mating or not.

When Dirk had finally exploded one night—after she'd lain frozen beneath him—she had exploded right back, telling him cruelly that if he couldn't give her a baby then she didn't want him any more. It had been a terrible thing to say, and she hadn't meant it at all. She'd regretted the words the moment they were out of her mouth.

She would never forget the awful stillness that had come over him, the almost frighteningly controlled fury in his face.

'Right,' he'd ground out, and turning, had stridden into the bedroom where he began packing.

She'd raced after him, panic-stricken. For beneath her insanity; her crazed behaviour; her apparent lack of desire for him as a man, she'd known she still loved him. He'd been all she'd ever wanted, right from the first moment she'd set eyes on him in that courtroom.

'Dirk, I'm sorry,' she'd insisted pleadingly. 'Please ... I ... I know I'm being awful. I'll be my old self again once I conceive. And it's only a matter of time. The doctor said there's nothing wrong with me, same as your doctor told you. He...he says I'm just too anxious. I need to relax and——'

Dirk's bitter laugh cut her off. 'Relax? Now that's a joke, Laura, and we both know it. Making love to you these days is like making love to a spring that's wound so tight, I'm almost afraid you'll snap if I touch you. Well, it's me who's snapped, my darling. I've had enough. I'm out of this marriage. Find yourself some other poor sucker to father this heaven-sent child you and that damned mother of yours so desperately want, because it certainly won't be me!'

Laura's guilt lessened as she once again remembered those last bitter words.

At first, they had torn into her very soul, making her feel wretched and extremely guilty. In fact it was this enormous guilt that had stopped her trying for a reconciliation with Dirk during the following weeks. She loved him and missed him dreadfully, but had been sure he was better off without her. Maybe he would be able to find some normal woman to marry who would fall pregnant with ease and not torment him with irrational behaviour. For she had felt certain that underneath his anger and frustration he'd also really wanted a child.

Her mother, however, had held a different opinion of what Dirk wanted from life.

'High-profile professional men like him don't really want children,' Vera had said with her usual cynicism. 'They live for their work. Women have only one part to play in their lives and we both know what *that* is. Babies are tolerated just to keep the little woman happy,' was her final scathing remark.

Laura hadn't agreed at all, and defended Dirk quite vehemently. That was why she had been so shattered when she found out a couple of months later that her mother had been right after all.

The occasion was etched into her mind forever. It was a week after Vera's sudden death from a coronary, and a few days after the funeral. Laura was home alone feeling devastated, a natural state of affairs since she'd been very close to her mother. They hadn't had any other relatives to fall back on, Vera being an orphan, and Laura her illegitimate and only child. Laura's father, an older and very wealthy playboy businessman, had abandoned her mother the moment he'd found out she was pregnant, his only offer of help being the money for an abortion. He'd died in a helicopter crash, apparently, when his daughter was two years old.

Dirk had always said Vera's experience had made her bitter and that she had filled Laura with warped ideas about men and sex. He'd once accused Laura of allowing her mother's brainwashing to taint their relationship, especially their sex life.

Though how he could say that she didn't know. Hadn't she gone to bed with him the very first night he'd taken her out, despite her virginal state? Hadn't she quickly surrender herself to his very passionate demands?

Sure, she'd been a little guilty, at first, at how easily he'd had his way with her. And she'd been worried, it was true, by her mother's constant warnings that a man like him only wanted her for her body. After all, he *was* ten years older than herself, an extremely handsome man and already a highly successful criminal lawyer, whereas she, at that time, was merely a sales assistant, her only claim to fame being a head of dark wavy hair, a pretty face and a shapely figure.

But Dirk had said he loved her, and within a few months they were married, much to her mother's annoyance and disapproval. Not that Laura had taken any notice of her ravings. By then she was so infatuated with Dirk and his expert lovemaking that her mother had had no chance at all of changing her mind about him.

'It's just sex,' Vera had kept insisting. 'Give it a year or two and he'll grow bored with you and want out. He won't let you have a baby. You mark my words!'

And he hadn't let her have a baby for the first year of their marriage, saying they needed time together before introducing a third party into their lives. But once she went off the Pill he had seemed genuinely thrilled when they thought she was pregnant with his child. But the test had proved negative and the doctor had explained that her missing periods were due to raised prolactin levels.

Yet even after this was remedied she had failed to conceive. For over a year, she'd remained optimistic and hopeful, but as month after anxious month kept going by her nerves had begun to fray and their relationship to crumble.

Making love had been reduced merely to a mechanical act to have a baby, done when the time was right, her temperature was right, even when her stars were right. It was madness. She had seen that as soon as Dirk left her. In the ghastly months that had followed she would have given anything to go back in time and undo all she had done.

At least ... that *had* been her wish, till Dirk had dropped his bombshell.

Laura's heart squeezed tight and she huddled further down in her seat. She'd been so happy to find him on her doorstep that awful day, so ridiculously happy...

'I'm really sorry about your mother,' he started after she'd invited him in for a cup of coffee. 'We didn't see eye to eye but I know she loved you, Laura. Maybe too much.'

'Yes,' she agreed, hope surging into her lonely, bereaved soul that he had come to see her because he wanted her back, because he thought maybe the time was right to try again. They hadn't seen each other, not once since the day after he'd stormed out, when he'd come back briefly to collect the rest of his things, telling her she could keep the unit and everything in it as well as the car he'd given her as a present.

That particular episode had been painfully awkward, with Dirk looking hard and grim, and she feeling too shattered and wretched to say a word in her own defence. Dirk's parting words had, in her opinion, sounded the death-knell on her marriage.

'When you decide you want a divorce, Laura, you know where to find me.'

Now here he was, mouthing soothing words over her mother's death and making her spirits soar as high as they possibly could during her time of bereavement.

Yet things only got worse...

'Dirk,' she started hesitatingly, her heart in her mouth. 'I've had a long time to think and I was hoping that...that...'

'That what, Laura?'

'That we might try again,' she blurted out.

He dragged in then expelled a ragged breath, and waited for an agonisingly long time before he spoke again.

'It wouldn't work,' he resumed with an edge to his voice. 'I can see it now. You'd start wanting a baby again and when you——' Suddenly, he broke off, frightening her with the hard resolve that slipped into his grey eyes. 'Look, I haven't come here today for a reconciliation. I'm enjoying my freedom far too much to want the chains of marriage hanging round my neck again. The reason for my visit, other than to offer my condolences, is to give you a piece of news that should please you.'

'P-please me?' Oh, God, he was going to ask for a divorce. And he thought that would *please* her?

'Yes. The fact is I've just discovered I'm sterile.'

Laura's mouth fell open in a silent gasp, her brain unable to make sense of what Dirk had just said. 'Sterile?' she repeated blankly.

'That's the correct term. I had a bout of mumps as a teenager which apparently killed off my sperm-making mechanism. So you see, given the right man, you'll probably fall pregnant quicker than a rabbit in springtime.'

She stared at him. 'But . . . but what about those tests you had?'

'I never had any done,' he confessed starkly.

'You . . . you never had any done . . . ?' She tried to swallow the enormous constriction that was forming in her chest. All those months of hoping and wanting, of unendurable wretchedness . . .

A bitter anguish swept through her. 'You *lied* to me? About something as important as that?'

He wasn't fazed by her accusatory tone. 'Not directly. I didn't think I needed to have the test done. There was this woman, you see . . . before I met you.' He shrugged carelessly. 'She said she was pregnant to me, and I had no reason to doubt it. When she had a convenient miscarriage, I was still left feeling confident of my potency. It wasn't till I ran into her recently and she admitted to trying to trap me into marriage that I began to wonder. So I had some tests done, and *voilá*! No little Xs and Ys at all, it seems.'

Laura couldn't take it all in—neither the bare fact of Dirk's sterility nor his incredibly flippant indifference to both it, and the pain he'd caused her. Was this the man who'd always said how much he loved her, who originally claimed he wanted a child as much as she did, who'd been able to put up with her irrational behaviour for ages till she'd driven him to distraction?

And then the penny dropped. He was covering up for his own despair. Not many men could cope with finding out they were incapable of fathering a child. She was sure Dirk would be no exception.

Hope clawed its way back into her heart. If only she could make him see it wasn't the end of the world, that she still loved him, no matter what. She lifted shining eyes and saw his face jerk back with surprise.

'But Dirk, I can deal with that,' she tried in desperation. 'I love you, don't you see? I've never stopped loving you. Your not being able to father a child doesn't mean we can't get back together or even eventually have children. There's artificial insemination, you know. I'm sure that after a few months I'd...'

He jumped to his feet, his face angry. 'My God, you're incredible, do you know that? Already you're thinking of a damned baby. Do you honestly think I'd put myself in such a position again, of watching you tear yourself into little pieces every month when the procedure failed? You must think I'm insane!'

He glared at her for a second before re-gathering his composure, adopting the coolly ruthless expression he used when he stood up to begin tearing a witness apart. 'Quite frankly, Laura, I don't want children anyway. I never really did. Neither do I want to resume our marriage, not in any circumstances. I'm free now, free to live the sort of life that suits me much better than marriage. Hell, I've got it made! As much sex as I want, with no unwanted packages to worry about.'

He laughed at her widening eyes. Actually laughed.

She rose slowly on shaky legs. 'Why on earth did you ever marry me in the first place?' she rasped.

His laughter was dry and cynical this time. 'There are all kinds of obsessions, dear heart, other than having a baby. I became obsessed with *you*. From the first moment I saw you in that witness box, your beautiful blue eyes defying me with their unimpeachable honesty...

'Hell,' he chuckled, 'I lost my case that day because I couldn't bear to cast doubt on your testimony. And I could have, believe me! In so many different ways. I could have painted you as a very young pretty salesgirl who spent most of her time chatting away to her fellow salesgirls and flirting with male customers, and couldn't possibly have been sure that my client was the same little old lady she thought she saw stuffing a blouse in her bag.

'Fortunately, my client was guilty, anyway. I only took her case as a favour to her son, who was a friend of mine. And there *were* extenuating circumstances. The poor old dear's husband had not long passed away and she was quite mentally disturbed. Luckily, her doctor's testimony assured she was let off with a bond, and my failure to discredit you didn't matter in the end. But, to be brutally honest, I was more concerned with catching up with you after the trial than with my client that day.

Never had a girl bewitched me so. You were an intriguing blend of moral strength, sweet innocence and the most appealing vulnerability. To be honest, I was prepared to do just about anything to have you, and keep on having you. Words of undying love... an engagement-ring... a wedding-ring... Even a baby. But the cost was too high in the end, my sweet. Far too high. Now I can happily tell you I've found a cure for *my* obsession. Best of luck with yours!'

His answer haunted her long after he'd gone. It haunted her now, in this darkened theatre, with its callous perpetrator sitting right behind her.

What kind of man was it that she had married?

The kind who had no conscience where sex was concerned, who would marry for lust, then walk out without a backward glance, who would flaunt another female in his wife's face, knowing she still loved him.

Laura felt her insides begin to shake with anger.

But worst of all was the way he'd looked at her out in that damned foyer, as though their separation had resurrected his once insatiable passion for her and he wouldn't mind going to bed with her again.

Hell would freeze over before she would let that bastard even *touch* her, Laura vowed fiercely.

But as the second half of the show rolled to its finale without her having watched a single moment Laura was tortured by the fact that hell was indeed what she'd been in ever since he'd set that sexually charged gaze upon her.

Hell, with all its fire and wickedness and temptations. The devil himself was in her mind, tempting her, reminding her of what it had once been like in Dirk's arms. The rapture...the abandonment...the sheer physical pleasure...

Hot blood began rushing back into her face. By the time the clapping finished and the lights came on, Laura was frightened to stand up, to turn round, to meet those smiling, seductive eyes once more.

Finally, she could sit there no longer. She rose jerkily, then turned.

The seats behind her were empty.

CHAPTER TWO

LAURA wandered through Morrie and Carmel's large living-room, regretting her decision to come to their post-première party. Despite the many groups of laughing, chatting people—most of them acquaintances of hers from the theatre group—she felt horribly alone. Not only that—the smoke-filled atmosphere was beginning to bother her.

Holding the glass of white wine Morrie had pressed into her hands a minute before, she made her way over to the heavily curtained french doors and slipped through them out on to the back patio. The evening air was quite fresh, but infinitely preferable to the stuffy air inside. Laura moved to stand at the top of the patio steps, sipping her drink and idly watching a cool April breeze ripple the surface of the pool down below.

She'd spent many a happy afternoon around that pool, with Dirk by her side...

Memories flooded back with a vengeance. Dirk teaching her how to swim and dive properly. Dirk sitting under that umbrella, helping her with her reading, encouraging her to overcome the dyslexia which had plagued her life. Dirk lying back in a deck-chair with the road-rule book in his hands, testing her over and over so that she could get her driving licence.

What had happened to that kind, caring Dirk? she wondered. Where was he these days?

The answer was pure and simple. No...not pure. Just simple. He was in bed with that brunette. And he wasn't having to teach her a thing!

Laura squeezed her eyes tightly shut against the pain that invaded her heart. She shouldn't have come here tonight. She really shouldn't have.

Yet now that she was here she couldn't bring herself to turn round and go home, back to her empty flat and her empty bed.

Sighing, she opened her eyes and moved on down the steps, through the child-proof gate and along to the far end of the pool, where she settled herself into one of the white plastic deck-chairs. Leaning back, her eyes automatically lifted to the back of the house and the row of bedroom windows along the top storey.

Only one was lit—the one on the end. Donna's bedroom, Laura realised, recalling from one of her previous visits that Carmel always left the light on because her seven-year-old daughter was afraid of the dark.

Laura smiled fondly as she thought of the shy, quiet but very sweet Donna, then grimaced as her mind went to Nicholas, Donna's four-year-old brother. What a holy little terror that boy was! Hypertensive, the doctor called him. Hypertensive, my eye! she thought. Spoilt rotten was Laura's opinion. And very self-willed. It would be a miracle if he grew safely to adulthood. As it was, he'd already broken several bones falling off roofs and out of trees, as well as nearly having drowned twice in this very pool, despite the security fence that surrounded it.

Still ... the child did have a certain charm, with his big blue eyes and blond curls and his oh, so ready smiles. He was an extrovert, just like his parents. Donna, by comparison, was not so physically attractive, with her long, straight mousy brown hair and smallish grey eyes. Neither was she outgoing by nature. She would always be socially overshadowed by her younger brother, which was why, perhaps, Laura had always favoured her. She did so hate it when children were praised and fussed over solely because of their looks. It wasn't fair.

Laura was mulling over this thought and staring rather blankly at Donna's window when a large, dark shadow moved in front of it. She jerked forward on the deck-chair, some of the wine spilling on her burgundy woollen culottes. But she didn't notice. Her attention was riveted on the black figure silhouetted against the lighted window.

A man. A very tall, large, dark man. Definitely not Morrie, who was only average in height, with a slight build.

Laura froze. The thought that a drunken male party-goer might have wandered into Donna's bedroom, even by mistake, filled her with alarm. The little girl would be terrified if she woke and found a stranger in her room, let alone ...

Visions of unspoken horrors spilled into Laura's mind.

She was on her feet and running in a flash, tipping the rest of the splashing wine into the pool as she went. Nerves made her fumble with the tricky lock on the pool gate, and she was glad no one was around to hear her swear. Once through the gate, she raced up the steps, across the patio and into the noisy, crowded living-room. Music had started up and people were dancing everywhere. Morrie and Carmel had to be there somewhere but she couldn't immediately see them. To stop and find them then have to explain the situation was a dangerous waste of time. Already Donna might be crying with fear. Or *worse*!

In no time Laura was flying up the stairs and along the dimly lit hall, bursting into the far end room with the wine glass held high, ready to attack this darkly perverse creature who dared enter a child's bedroom in the dead of night.

To see Donna sitting up in bed as bold as brass and right as rain rather took the wind out of Laura's sails. As did the sight of her errant husband sitting on his niece's bed, with a story-time book open on his lap.

His handsome blond head jerked up at her dramatic entrance, his left eyebrow arching sardonically as cool grey eyes swept over her high colour and heaving breasts.

'Aunty *Laura*!' Donna gasped, looking startled.

Dirk didn't look startled, merely drily amused.

'I wouldn't have thought you'd be so anxious to see me again tonight,' he drawled.

Laura gripped the wine glass lest she hurl it across the room at his supercilious face.

'I was sitting beside the pool,' she said through gritted teeth, 'when I saw a man at Donna's window, so I . . . I . . .'

'So you came to rescue our fair damsel here,' he finished for her, 'with sword drawn to the ready.' And he nodded at the fluted glass, which was still raised in attack mode.

Laura's fingers tightened around it again in fury at Dirk's mocking attitude. But no sooner had she decided she hated him more than anyone else in the world than his expression softened to one of true admiration.

'You are many things, my darling Laura,' he murmured, 'but never a coward.'

Donna's little face beamed with joy as she looked from one of them to the other. 'Have you and Aunty Laura made up, Uncle Dirk? Oh, I'm so happy! I did so miss Aunty Laura coming to visit with you.'

Laura's heart turned over with dismay. She hadn't realised before how her separation from Dirk might have affected the sensitive little girl.

Oh, God, I'm a selfish cow, she groaned silently. Not for a moment did I think of what Donna might be feeling when I never came to visit any more.

Laura grimaced. She didn't mean to be unaware of other people's feelings, knowing this was a result of being an only child with no brothers and sisters to consider—or a father for that matter; only a mother who doted on her.

But that was no excuse, she decided, and resolved then and there to visit Donna every so often, even if she had to put up with running into Dirk. At least she wouldn't have to face another of his women, since Carmel had forbidden them access to her home.

Meanwhile, she had to set the little girl straight about Dirk and herself as kindly as possible.

'Well, we haven't exactly made up, Donna,' she said gently. 'But we *are* trying to be polite to one another, aren't we, Dirk?'

Again that sardonic eyebrow lifted. 'Whatever you say. I'm a very amenable fellow.'

Laura just stopped herself in time from pulling a sour face at him, choosing instead a sick-looking smile.

'Then you can stay and listen to the rest of my story, Aunty Laura?' Donna chimed in.

To refuse would negate all she had tried to do so far. But, to be honest, Laura did not want to stay. There was something about the way Dirk kept looking at her that was sending a prickling up and down her spine. It was far too damned sexual. Far too knowing, as though he was well aware she still wanted him, and he found the idea both intriguing and amusing at the same time.

Her blue eyes tried to remain distant and cool as she returned his blatantly inquisitive stare. 'Why not?' she tossed off nonchalantly, and, putting the wine glass down, closed the bedroom door and walked forward. 'What story is it?' she asked Donna.

'*Red Riding Hood.*'

'Ah . . . my favourite.' Laura smiled down at the earnest little face.

'You can sit here, Aunty Laura,' the child offered, and patted the side of the bed not yet occupied.

Laura didn't want to be in the same *room* as Dirk, let alone sitting on the same bed, but instinct warned her not to give him any inkling of her discomfort. You didn't give a shark the smell of blood if you wanted to keep him at a safe distance.

'Isn't this a new quilt?' she remarked as she sat down.

'Yes,' Donna sighed. 'Nicholas has a new one too. It's got racing cars on it. He says his is better than mine.' Her face scrunched up into a disgruntled frown.

'I much prefer fairies and flowers to racing cars,' Laura pronounced, and Donna smiled with relief.

'What did I tell you, sweetie?' Dirk joined in. 'Girls and boys like different things. It doesn't mean either quilt is better than the other. Nick's only four. He doesn't understand such things yet. You have to be patient with him, since you're much more grown up.'

'Am I really, Uncle Dirk?'

'You sure are. Why, in no time you'll be a beautiful grown-up lady like your Aunty Laura.'

'Oh, I hope so,' Donna sighed again. 'She's really beautiful.'

'She sure is,' Dirk agreed, slanting Laura a look that might have caused spontaneous combustion if she hadn't had firm control over herself. Still, it took all her composure not to react when his eyes slid down the front of her cream satin blouse to linger on the thrust of her full breasts. She stared coolly back at him, and it was at that moment Laura noticed he wasn't wearing the tie he'd had on earlier tonight. Three buttons of his white silk shirt were also undone, showing a smattering of soft blond curls on his tanned chest.

The mental image of his tie having been left beside the brunette's bed popped into her mind.

Her eyes snapped back up to his, and once again he smiled at her as he had across the foyer. If Donna hadn't been present, looking at both of them with a happy, expectant face, Laura might have slapped him right then and there.

Instead, she smiled sweetly and said, 'Shouldn't we be getting on with the story, Dirk? It's getting late.'

He seemed to have to drag his eyes away from her body, leaving Laura far more rattled than she wanted to admit, even to herself.

I refuse to keep loving him, she repeated over and over in her mind. I definitely do not want him any more. I *despise* him!

And who do you think you're kidding? came a brutally honest voice from deep inside.

One would have thought that the simple reading of *Red Riding Hood* could not have made the situation any worse. But Dirk seemed to be able to put an underlying and very adult meaning into every second sentence.

'... and the big bad wolf smacked his lips and said, "All the better to *eat* you with, my dear..."'

When he delivered this little gem with an X-rated glance at her mouth, Laura had to will herself not to blush, lifting her chin slightly, and putting a sardonic curl on her lips. Just as well he couldn't hear the way her pulse-rate had picked up, or see the images that were dancing about in her mind.

Dirk had been a very imaginative and uninhibited lover in their early days.

Somehow she made it through to the end of the story. But when Donna asked her uncle to read the next one as well—*Goldilocks*—Laura was forced to object. The mind boggled at what Dirk would do with such lines as things being too hard and too soft, not to mention the 'Who's been sleeping in my bed?' bit.

'I think it's time for you to go to sleep, Donna,' she put in quite firmly. 'Your parents would not be too pleased with us keeping you up at this hour. You don't want us to get into trouble, do you?'

'N-no...'

'Well, then, your uncle can put the book away while I tuck you in and kiss you goodnight.'

'Oh, all right.'

Laura threw Dirk a challenging look, half expecting him to disagree. But he merely shrugged and stood up, reminding Laura just what a powerfully built man he was. From the look of him, he'd been working out at the gym even more than he used to.

Her eyes lifted to admire the breadth of his shoulders, and the way his torso came in narrow at the waist and hips. There was a time when she used to like running her fingers over his naked body as he lay sleeping, exploring the shape of him, though he would inevitably wake beneath her gently wandering hands, urging her to stronger and far more erotic ministrations.

Suddenly, he turned around and caught her staring at him with the glitter of remembered desire in her gaze. She dropped her eyes back to Donna. But too late, she thought. Too late...

'I love you, Aunty Laura,' Donna whispered when she bent to kiss her.

'And I love you too, darling,' she returned softly, a churning in her stomach. 'Would you like it if I came to visit soon?'

'Oh, *yes!*'

'Then I will. I promise. Now off to sleep.'

Donna was already yawning by the time Dirk and Laura left the room. No sooner had they closed the door behind them than Laura let fly with some of the anger that had been smouldering inside her all night.

'I certainly didn't appreciate the sickeningly pathetic *double entendres* you put into that story, Dirk. I found them tacky and tasteless.'

He pushed his suit jacket open and slid his hands into his trouser pockets, the action pulling the dark grey material tight over his trim hips and long, muscular thighs. 'Really? I found them rather amusing myself.'

'You would,' she scoffed. 'And I also don't like the sort of looks you've been giving me tonight. I suggest you stay a bit longer with your brunette in future. You've obviously never got over your need for seconds!'

His laughter was brittle. 'I was hard pushed to get to *firsts* with you, Laura, honey, towards the end. But there was a time,' he went on in a more teasing tone, 'when you were only too happy with giving me thirds. Even fourths.'

A fierce heat stole into her cheeks. 'Why are you doing this, Dirk?' she said, shaken by her response to mere words. 'What is it that you want of me?'

'Want of you, Laura?' His expression was one of bland innocence, giving her no clue as to what was going on within that darkly devious mind of his. 'I want nothing from you except what you're willing to give me. Tonight, I'll settle for your company at the party downstairs.'

'*Tonight*?' Her own laughter was half startled, half sarcastic. 'You talk as if there might be *other* nights for us!'

His smile, when it came, was decidedly wicked. 'Let's take one night at a time, shall we?'

Stunned, she shook her head in disbelief. 'You must be mad! We're finished, Dirk. Well and truly finished. I didn't realise that fully till tonight when I actually saw you with that woman. My feelings for you are finally dead!'

'Dead, Laura?'

His hands slid out of his pockets and lifted to snake around her neck, thumbs along her jaw, fingers spreading under the thick glossy waves that fell heavily to her shoulders. Laura's whole skin broke out into goose-bumps. She supposed she should have moved or done something, but her eyes were locked to his and she seemed unable to break away from their steely and somewhat hypnotic spell.

'I don't think so,' he taunted softly. 'I don't think so at all...'

When his mouth began to descend, Laura snapped out of it. 'If you kiss me,' she rasped, 'I'll kick you.'

'Good,' was his cryptic comment.

He did kiss her. And she did kick him. Hard. On the shins—but several seconds after she should have, which made her kick him all the harder; she was so mad at herself.

He gave little reaction to her vicious kick other than a grunt and a savage grasping of the hair at the nape of her neck. Next thing she knew she was swung round and pressed hard against the opposite wall, imprisoned there by his outspread legs and a chest that was large and wide and impregnable. Her hands were free, but dangled uselessly by her side, her shoulders and elbows pinned back by the width of his upper body. Her head couldn't move an inch, solidly captured by his merciless grip of both his large, strong hands.

'Don't kick me, Laura,' he urged in a hot, husky voice. 'Kiss me instead. Take your fury and frustration out on my mouth, not my shins.'

Laura's head whirled as his lips took possession of hers once more, her thoughts confusing her. She could not believe that she still loved and wanted this man so much, certainly could not understand why she was finding this display of sheer male forcefulness so exciting. She would have thought such actions would have repelled her. But rather than being repelled, she was actually revelling in the feel of his hard hands around her face, in the way he was prising her lips open seemingly against her will.

Of course Dirk would never physically hurt her. Somewhere in the back of Laura's mind lay that security, that absolute certainty. Why she felt sure of that was somewhat of a mystery. Perhaps it was because during the last few months of their life together, no matter how angry Dirk got with her, how frustrated, he had never hit her or tried to force sex on her.

A sensual moan sighed in her throat when her lips were finally forced apart and his tongue drove deep. He gave an echoing moan, his hands splaying up into her hair, fingertips pressing into her scalp as he turned her head from side to side. Kiss followed kiss, with Laura quickly abandoning her pose of uninvolved submission. Her own long-suppressed desires and needs would not be denied and she began kissing him back with a wild, desperate hunger.

'Hey! Who's that down there?'

Dirk took his time releasing her mouth, giving her a heavy-lidded and highly satisfied look before turning to face his brother.

'It's only me, Morrie,' he said lazily.

'For God's sake, Dirk,' his brother snapped as
he strode down the hall towards them. 'What the
hell do you think you're doing? I thought
you——' He broke off abruptly when he saw who
it was flattened against the wall, face flushed,
breasts rising and falling with betraying speed.
'*Laura*?' His mouth flapped open, wide eyes going
from Dirk to Laura then back to Dirk. 'Well, well,
well. Have you two finally—er——?'

'No,' Dirk supplied succinctly, and stepped away
from Laura. 'We haven't.'

'But...' Morrie threw her a frowning glance.

Laura decided she was incapable of explaining a
thing at that moment. The colour in her cheeks was
not just the result of arousal, but of shame too.
Dark, bitter shame. God, she was a weak, stupid,
vulnerable idiot without a single scrap of personal
pride and dignity!

Fancy having allowed Dirk to do that to her, and
with such incredible ease. He'd said it all with his
smugly triumphant look. And how could she have
been such a fool as to challenge his male ego by
saying her feelings for him were dead when she
knew damned well *he* knew they weren't? Hadn't
she betrayed them every darned time she saw him?
Now she had shown him in the most explicit way
that she was still his for the taking, if and when he
chose to take her.

Her only defence was to get herself away from
him, and to stay away from him. Out of sight was
out of mind, at least where *he* was concerned. Laura
didn't think he would pursue her. He'd run into her

tonight by accident, decided he still fancied her a bit and had taken full advantage of her ongoing and obvious desire for him. Her only small satisfaction was that he couldn't be sure she still loved him. She vowed that no matter what happened she would never admit to that. And very soon, with a bit of luck, it wouldn't even be so!

Levering herself away from the wall, she lanced her husband with a bitter look. 'I'll let you explain to your brother that what he saw was nothing,' she bit out. 'Less than nothing, really. It's amazing what a couple of glasses of wine can do to normally sensible females. They end up kissing a man they patently despise. Bye, Morrie. It was a nice party, up to a point. Tell Carmel I'll ring her soon.'

With head held high, she turned and walked away, holding herself together till she was in her car and on her way home, even then refusing to cry. He wasn't worth tears. He was a bastard, a devil, a two-timer and a liar!

But when she closed her front door and looked around the spacious, elegantly furnished unit she'd once shared happily with him, and which now seemed so cold and empty and sad, something broke inside her. Her back slid down the door till she was sitting in a wretched huddle on the floor. Her head drooped forward on to her knees and finally she started to sob.

CHAPTER THREE

LAURA hopped off her train at Central on the Monday morning and made her way quickly to the Eddy Street exit, running down the steep steps to the street below. The weather was overcast and cool, with a brisk wind whistling down the city streets. Not at all pleasant.

On mornings like this she wished she could drive to work in the comfort of her air-conditioned Ford Laser, but parking around here was far too much of a problem. Besides, it was much quicker by train from her unit at Milson's Point, and her office was only a five-minute walk from the station.

Laura rushed to join the throng of workers waiting at the corner for the lights to change. They pinged to green and the group surged forward, heads down, feet scurrying. The North Shore train line had been running a bit late and it was already ten to nine—not long to go if one had to be sitting at one's desk at nine.

Laura was supposed to be at hers at eight-thirty, but the morning had not gone well, right from the moment she woke to realise she hadn't set her alarm the previous evening. Then she'd discovered a stain on the skirt of her black serge suit after she'd put it on, and with no time to waste she'd changed into her royal-blue jersey dress—a regular stand-by if she needed to wear something without having to even *look* at an iron.

But she was frowning over her choice of dress as she hurried up the steep pavement towards Fenwick Fashions. It was a touch cool to wear on a chilly autumn day, with only elbow-length sleeves. She really should have worn her grey suit, and perhaps would have if she hadn't mislaid the belt that went with it. No doubt it was on the floor of her wardrobe somewhere, along with a whole pile of other 'lost' things. Truly, she would have to tidy that disaster area soon.

Laura sighed. Tidiness was not one of her greatest virtues, having had a mother who had done everything for her at home. Then, when she'd married Dirk, a cleaner had come in twice a week. Now, with the cleaner having gone the same way Dirk had, she had to do all her own washing and cleaning and ironing, and had never quite got the hang of being organised or dedicated to housework. She much preferred creative pastimes such as sewing, as evidenced by her dining table being littered with half-made outfits and patterns draped over the back of chairs.

But what did it matter, she thought defensively, if she was a little untidy? There was no one to see it. Or care.

This thought resurrected the sort of feelings that had brought bouts of crying the whole of Sunday, and Laura felt her chin begin to tremble once more.

Not again, she lectured herself sternly, and gulped down the lump in her throat. As it is, you look as if you've been out on the tiles all weekend, with dark rings under your eyes. How would it look if you walked into the office with tears and mascara running down your cheeks? What would all your colleagues think?

'Never wear your heart on your sleeve,' her mother had always told her. 'Smile and the world smiles with you. Cry and you cry alone.'

'Well, I was certainly crying alone yesterday, Mum,' she muttered aloud. 'And it didn't feel too good. And now I'm talking to myself. A sure sign of insanity!'

Sighing, she turned into the ancient, two-storeyed square brick building that was the head office of Fenwick Fashions, drumming up a smile as she passed Reception. She didn't stop to go to the ladies' room as she usually did, hurrying across the lobby instead into the office she shared with Hester, the other head buyer.

For a moment she thought Hester wasn't there either, but when she closed the door Hester popped up from where she'd been crouched down behind her desk. A svelte and beautiful blonde in her early thirties, she was much more experienced in the fashion world than Laura. Consequently, Laura had never got over the habit of always deferring to Hester as though she were her boss instead of an equal.

'I'm sorry I'm late,' she said hastily. 'My alarm didn't go off and the train was late and——'

Hester's soft laughter stopped her flow of excuses. 'Heavens, Laura, you don't have to apologise. In all the months we've been working together you've never once been late. I think Fenwick Fashions will excuse you this one time, don't you? Especially since you're always working late these days and taking work home without expecting overtime pay.'

Laura smiled weakly, at the same time dragging in then expelling a ragged breath. 'Yes, I suppose so...' Moving over to her desk, she dropped her handbag beside it and slumped down into her chair, painfully aware of Hester's frowning eyes upon her.

'Anything wrong, Laura?' her colleague asked. 'You look pale. Aren't you well?'

Laura tried to smile, but it felt shaky round the edges. 'I'll be all right by tomorrow. It's that time of the month.'

'But that doesn't usually affect you adversely, does it? You never take days off from work like some of the other girls around here—me included.'

'Maybe I'm a little run-down,' Laura sighed, wishing she hadn't brought the subject up.

Hester was right, of course. Laura didn't suffer from pain or discomfort with her period. It was usually blessedly light and only lasted a few days. But its arrival yesterday had been bad timing, coming the day after her upsetting encounter with Dirk. She'd been emotionally distressed as it was, without a reminder that she would never have what she had once wanted most in the world: Dirk's baby.

Not that having his child seemed so important any more. She would have settled for having her old Dirk back, baby or no baby. But the incidents on Saturday night had proved once and for all that the Dirk she had married was gone forever.

If he'd ever existed in the first place...

A very real anguish seized Laura's heart. It was so hard to accept the truth, to believe that her Prince Charming had been no more than a figment of her naïve imagination. Or alternatively Dirk had just been a good actor, prepared to play the role of adoring, attentive husband so that he could have what he wanted: *her*, in his bed every night.

'You know, Laura,' Hester said softly, 'if you ever need to talk, *I'm* here. And I don't gossip.'

Laura's clouded expression cleared to one of surprise as she glanced over at her colleague. She didn't quite know how to respond to this unexpected offer. Despite the amount of time they spent together, she and Hester had never shared confidences of a private nature. 'Oh—er—thanks, Hester. I... I'll remember that.'

Hester's smile was vaguely sad, as though she pitied Laura.

Feeling oddly uncomfortable, Laura was almost relieved when Claudia came through the door with the mail, even if it was without knocking—something both Hester and herself hated.

'And how are we all this morning?' Claudia asked, sweeping her eagle eyes over both of them, then zeroing in on Laura like a homing pigeon. 'My, my, my...' She walked over to stand on the other side of the desk, peering more closely at Laura's face. 'Did we have a heavy weekend? That's not like you, Laura. Don't tell me you've finally found someone to replace that womanising husband of yours?'

Her laughter was like chalk on a blackboard to Laura. 'Still...you might as well. My sources tell me he has another new dolly-bird—a sultry actress by the unlikely name of Virginia.'

'Oh, for pity's sake. Claudia,' Hester snapped most uncharacteristically. 'Just drop the mail and go, will you? I would have thought you'd have better things to do than gossip about Laura's ex, especially since the summer orders have to be completed by the end of this week.'

'Well, pardon me for breathing, I'm sure!' Claudia humphed. '*Some* people find it natural to discuss their weekend with their co-workers on a Monday morning. *Others* are incorrigible snobs who never have a friendly or kind word for anyone!' And, with a savagely pointed glare at Laura, she stormed out of the office, slamming the door behind her.

Laura stared after her, mouth agape.

'Don't take any notice of her,' Hester said dismissively.

Laura shook her head. 'I just don't know why she hates me so much. I mean...I know she resented my getting promoted over her at the beginning of last year, but it seems to run deeper than that.'

'Oh, I don't know...'

Laura detected a reluctance on Hester's part to discuss the subject, which rather contradicted her earlier offer of a closer relationship.

'Tell me the truth, Hester,' she said firmly. 'Do I come across as a snob to the other girls?'

Hester sighed. 'Look, I——'

'The truth,' Laura broke in. '*Please.*'

Her colleague sighed. 'A little bit, maybe. You—er—don't ever go out into the tea-room and chat with the other women, so you've never satisfied their female curiosity over your marriage and its break-up.'

'Oh, come on,' Laura defended herself. 'Surely I couldn't be expected to tell everyone a blow-by-blow description of my private life? *You* don't do that!'

'*I'm* not married to Dirk Thornton.'

Laura frowned in confusion.

'You must realise, Laura, that your husband became quite a celebrity after he got that poor battered wife off with a self-defence plea. That murder trial, and his movie-star looks, made him a sort of romantic ideal to lots of women in Australia, and *you* were married to him. Do you see what I mean? They wanted to hear about him. Most of them felt sorry for you when he left you, and wanted to express their sympathy, but you didn't give them the opportunity. Even when your mother died, you sort of froze people out around here with your stiff-upper-lip, no-tears-at-the-office attitude.'

'I see,' Laura mumbled. And she did see, feeling numbed by the same wretched realisation she'd come to on Saturday night with Donna. She was blind to the feelings of others. Totally blind.

'Hey, don't look like that,' Hester soothed. 'It's not all your fault. You're naturally a reserved person, and Claudia—for want of a better word—is a right bitch!'

'I . . . I never was good at making friends,' Laura tried to explain. 'Even at school. I had this problem with reading, you see, and the other girls used to make fun of me over it. They made me feel stupid and different so I spent most of my life growing up without friends and without learning how to *be* a friend. And now, even though I've got much more confidence in myself, I guess I've never got out of the habit of keeping myself to myself where other women are concerned.'

Hester's smile was wry. 'As I've already said, Laura, don't be so hard on yourself. Have you ever stopped to think that a woman who looks like you isn't likely to have many female friends anyway?'

Laura was taken aback. 'Looks like me? But I'm not that good-looking. You're *far* more attractive than I am!'

'In a coldly two-dimensional, feature-by-feature comparison I probably am. But you've got a certain something, Laura, that men find very appealing, and it goes deeper than your looks. Maybe it's that air of untouchability you wear around them. Oh, you can laugh, but you should see some of the randy, frustrated looks the reps give you when you're not looking, as though they're dying to make a pass but have no idea how to go about it.

Sometimes I wonder if they give you such good discounts because they're hoping to score with you.'

Laura merely shook her head in amazement.

A tap on their office door brought an end to their chat, especially when a perfectly strange young man popped his head inside.

'Mrs Thornton?' he enquired from the doorway, looking from one woman to the other. 'Mrs Laura Thornton?'

'That's me,' Laura admitted with a small frown of puzzlement.

'Flowers for you,' he announced, and bounced into the room with the most exquisite floral arrangement in a basket that Laura had ever seen. She literally gaped as it was placed on her desk, her blue eyes widening as she counted over a dozen red roses, and even more red carnations, as well as other assorted yellow-gold flowers and lots of baby's breath.

'Got quite an admirer here, lady,' the courier grinned, then bounced out again only to return with a second basket, this one full of pink roses and carnations complemented by white daisies and wispy fronds of emerald-green fern.

'Is that it?' Laura asked breathlessly.

'Gees, lady. Do you want more?' And with a parting grin he was gone.

Laura stared at the flowers, her thoughts in disarray. Who could have sent them? One of those secret admirers Hester was just telling her about?

The answer slipped into her mind like a venomous snake, making her shudder. Dirk...

'Aren't you going to look at the cards?' Hester asked as she came over to inspect the magnificent blooms at close range. 'Oh, aren't they gorgeous? Laura, if you don't tell me who they're from this very second I'm going to agree with Claudia and call you every name in the book!'

'They're from Dirk,' she said, and gave another shiver. Why was he doing this? *Why*?

'How can you be sure without looking at the cards?' Hester argued.

'I just can. But you can read them if you like.'

'Really?' Hester looked both startled and delighted. But she didn't hesitate. 'This first one says, *"My humblest apologies. I was way out of line."* Oh, what *did* he do? And the next one is... Oh, my goodness...'

Laura's eyes snapped up. 'What? What does it say?'

'It says, *"If I'm forgiven, join me for dinner this Friday night at Kable's. 8p.m."*'

Laura gasped with outrage. 'My God! Just like that! And he probably expects me to show up!'

'After he's spent a small fortune on all these flowers, I would imagine so,' the other woman concluded drily.

'Of all the nerve!' Laura sat there, grinding her teeth and glaring at the flowers, before suddenly frowning up at Hester.

'You've never been married, have you, Hester?'

'No, but I'm not unacquainted with the male sex. I'm living with one of its lesser specimens at the moment,' she finished with an ironic little smile.

'*Are* you?' For a second Laura was distracted to think of this cool, classical beauty putting up with any less than perfection in a man. Not that *she* could talk, after what Dirk had done to her—what he was *still* trying to do to her! But she needed to hear the ugly truth from someone else's lips.

'If I tell you what happened last Saturday night,' she began, 'would you give me your objective and honest advice?'

'Love to,' Hester said, eyes glittering with curiosity as she perched herself on the corner of Laura's desk. 'Shoot.'

Five minutes later, she was pulling a face and mulling over Laura's final question, clearly unwilling to put her thoughts into words.

'Well?' Laura prompted at last. 'Don't be tactful. Tell me what you think Dirk wants.'

'You want it straight?'

'Of course.'

'First of all, give me a clue as to why you think he left you in the first place. Was it other women then or something else?'

Laura opened her mouth then closed it again. Much as she was appreciating having someone to talk her problem over with, she felt there was a line she had to draw, preferring to keep really private things private. So she came up with an answer that was basically true, but not too revealing.

'The crux of it was, Hester,' she said, 'Dirk didn't want children and I did. Although, from what he's told me since, even if the issue of children hadn't

come up I think he still would have tired of me
eventually and left anyway.'

'Mmm . . . Yes, there are some men who can't be
monogamous. They're just not made that way. And
I think your Dirk is one of them. So, if that's the
case, the answer to your question is obvious, Laura.
I hate to say this, since you're clearly still in love
with the man, but all he wants from you is sex.'

Laura's insides contracted with both distaste and
a bitter dismay. Which was crazy, since that was
the conclusion she had already come to herself.
How long would it take for her foolish heart to let
go the old false image of Dirk?

'I'm afraid I'm forced to agree with you,' she
said tautly.

'So what are you going to do? Surely you're not
going to go to dinner with him, are you? It's quite
obvious who's on the menu for afters.'

Laura stood up and picked up the baskets of
flowers, deciding on the spot that she would have
them sent down to the children's hospital at
Camperdown. She couldn't bear to look at them,
but neither could she bring herself to throw such
beautiful flowers away.

Her eyes were cold and bleak as she faced Hester
across the desk. 'I don't think so, Hester. I won't
be staying that long. But I *am* going to show up.
I'm going to look right into that handsome, treach-
erous face of his and do what I should have done
months ago: tell the rotter that I want a divorce!'

CHAPTER FOUR

'MRS THORNTON?'

Laura glanced up at the waiter. 'Yes?' she said, aware that her sharp tone was betraying her irritation.

But it was hard not to be irritated. She had arrived at the Regent Hotel in a taxi, suitably late at eight-fifteen, and dressed in her freshly dry-cleaned but clearly no-nonsense black serge suit, ready to give Dirk a piece of her mind. She'd even put her hair up in a chignon and kept her make-up light so that her total look was cool and businesslike.

And what had happened? When she'd swept up the staircase to present herself at Kable's, Dirk wasn't waiting for her as she had anticipated. All that was waiting for her was a message that he had been delayed, that he would be with her shortly and that she was to order a cocktail or two till then.

Three daiquiris later, the waiter was hovering next to her, an anxious look on his face. 'Mr Thornton apologises once more, madam, but he is still detained and has advised me to request you proceed with your meal until he arrives.'

'Does he, now?' Her voice was tight with a growing agitation.

'Yes, madam.' The waiter looked disconsolate, and Laura thought what a splendid actor he was.

51

But then most of the waiters around Sydney *were* out-of-work, aspiring actors. They were also often very good-looking young men. This one certainly was, being tall and dark with piercing black eyes. If he was overdoing the concerned act a bit, it *was*, after all, only part of his job.

Suddenly, she grinned up at him and before he could stop himself he grinned back. His perfectly straight, dazzling white teeth showed either good genes or a good dentist.

'Very well, Jonathan. That is your name, isn't it? Jonathan?' She'd heard the *maître d'* call him that.

'Yes, madam.' He tried to recover his po-faced dignity but she could see the corners of his mouth twitching.

'I think at this point in time I'll skip the entrée and head straight into the main course. Now what do you suggest . . . ?' And she picked up the menu that had been lying on the table in front of her for nearly an hour.

Less than fifteen minutes later, Laura was tackling a magnificent fillet of barramundi, swathed in a delicious sauce, accompanied by a lightly tossed salad and a crispy bread roll. The daiquiris had given way to a bottle of exquisite Chardonnay that was so expensive, it was obscene.

But then, *she* wasn't paying for it, Laura thought with bitter relish.

She was just devouring the last morsel of fish when her heart gave a little leap. Dirk was striding across the floor of the restaurant towards her, looking very suave and debonair in a three-piece navy blue pin-stripe suit. The overhead lights made his thick, glossy hair look more silver than blond, which only added to his air of urbane sophistication. He looked every inch the magnificent man in the prime of his life that he was.

Laura tried not to care that every woman in the place stopped what she was doing to watch him pass by. But, to give him credit, his eyes were all for her, as was his practised smile of apology when he sat down opposite and flicked out his white linen serviette.

'I'm so sorry, Laura; I was caught up soothing an important witness who had a very bad afternoon in the dock. But I knew you'd understand.'

'Did you, Dirk?' she said coldly. 'A woman witness, no doubt?'

He smiled. 'Yes, as a matter of fact.'

Just as he hadn't bothered to hide his amusement, so Laura didn't bother to hide her sarcasm. 'Quite understandable, then. Women witnesses *do* take considerable soothing, I'm sure. The only thing I *don't* understand,' she lashed out tartly, 'is why you assumed I'd turn up tonight at *all*, let alone wait for you for over an hour.'

His grey eyes remained amused as they roved over her stiffly reproachful face. 'But you did wait, didn't you?'

'I would have waited twenty-four hours to say what I have to say,' came her acid retort.

The muscles tightening in his neck showed some reaction to her hostility, but his eyes looked untroubled as they held hers. Damn it, but he had the best poker-face in the world when he wanted! Laura knew she didn't have a hope in Hades of guessing what he was really thinking, or how her news would affect him.

'That sounds ominous,' he said lightly. 'Can I get myself a drink before you give me the pronouncement of doom?'

When she shrugged offhandedly he signalled the waiter and ordered a triple Scotch on the rocks.

'One would hope you're not driving home later,' she said sharply. 'It's been raining and the roads are slippery. If you drink the way you used to on a Friday night, you'll probably end up having an accident.'

'Would you care if I did?'

The image of him wrapped around a telegraph pole didn't give her any pleasure. Which was surprising.

'Yes,' she said with a rueful honestly. 'I would.'

He seemed surprised, but pleased. 'In that case, I'll share your taxi.'

'You will *not*!'

'No? Why not?'

'I think you know very well why not! Do you really think I don't know where this is all supposed to be heading, Dirk? First your smarmy looks last Saturday night, not to mention that disgusting kiss. Then the flowers, and now dinner.'

He managed to contrive an almost innocent expression. 'Well, you know more than me, then. Where *is* this supposed to be heading?

'Bed, of course!'

His eyebrows shot up. 'Is it? By God and I forgot to change the sheets this morning. Well, it will have to be your place, darling, won't it? Can I stay till morning? Do you have my favourite brand of coffee in stock?'

Her upper lip curled with contempt as she surveyed his handsome, mocking face. 'Very droll, Dirk. Very droll. I made it quite clear last Saturday night that I don't want anything further to do with you.'

'Which is why you're here tonight?' he taunted softly.

'I'm here tonight for one reason and one reason only: to look you in the face and tell you I want a divorce. As quickly as possible.'

His eyes didn't flicker, though he did take a while to respond verbally. 'How tiresome,' he drawled. 'All that paperwork. Are you sure you wouldn't prefer to just live with him?'

Laura sighed. 'There is no *him*, Dirk. Believe it or not, I don't want a divorce to marry again. I just don't want to be known as Mrs Dirk Thornton any more! Quite frankly, it's humiliating, with the multitude of women you've been seen running around with.'

He laughed. 'And there I was thinking I was being discreet. But fair enough. I'll get to it first thing Monday morning. Do you trust me to do it or do you want to hire your own solicitor as well?'

Laura blinked. Just like that? OK, here's your divorce, honey. Bye?

Her hand trembled slightly as she picked up her glass and emptied it in one deep swallow. Why was she so upset? Had she expected him to argue with her, to say he *wouldn't* give her a divorce?

'I don't trust you as far as I can throw you, Dirk. My solicitor will be in touch.'

His face fell with mock distress. 'Oh, Laura . . . I'm crushed . . .'

'Well, your suit certainly isn't,' she shot back, eyeing the splendid fit of the jacket across his broad shoulders with considerable pique. Why did men like Dirk never look crumpled, or out of sorts, or simply lousy? Why did they always look smooth and sleek and totally in control?

'You like my suit?' he grinned. 'It's new and all Australian-made. So you can't accuse of me of being unpatriotic. And I presume that's a Fenwick Fashion creation you're wearing?'

'Yes,' she said shortly.

His patrician nose wrinkled. 'It's a bit severe, isn't it? I like my women to dress in softer-styled garments.'

'Yes,' she bit out. 'I know.'

He stared at her for second, then smiled one of those slow, devastatingly knowing smiles that would make any woman's toes curl up. Laura was no exception, but at least her toes were safely hidden in shoes under the table.

She returned his smile with a smile of her own. It was cold and contemptuous.

'You really shouldn't challenge me, Laura,' came his low, lazy warning.

The waiter materialised at their table at this fortuitous moment, allowing Laura to regroup her defences from the inside out. It was wickedly unfair that any man could be that damned sexy. One charged look from Dirk and all her circuits were in danger of being scrambled.

'Your drink, sir,' the waiter announced, and placed the glass of Scotch neatly by Dirk's right hand before moving swiftly around the table to scoop the bottle of Chardonnay up from the silver ice-bucket. With white-gloved hand and deft movements he refilled Laura's glass then replaced the bottle.

'Thank you, Jonathan,' she murmured automatically once he'd finished.

'My pleasure, madam.' The warm lilt in the waiter's voice drew her eyes upwards and they exchanged a quick smile.

'*Jonathan*?' Dirk said archly once the waiter was out of earshot. 'You certainly aren't as shy with people as you used to be, dear Laura. Unless you were already acquainted with dear Jonathan before you came here tonight.'

Laura turned icy blue eyes her husband's way. She hadn't missed the caustic edge to his comments, as though he hadn't been pleased by what had just happened. She found his jealousy laughable, given the circumstances.

'I won't answer that last pathetic remark. As for my shyness . . . yes, I'm gradually getting over that. I still lack social skills in certain situations, but I think I've grown this past year. Hurt and hardship either make or break people. I'd like to think I'm the former result.'

For several moments their eyes locked, his a cold, steely grey, hers a vibrant, angry blue.

Dirk broke the clash of wills with a wry smile. 'I'm sure you are. So... you haven't found your dream man yet? The one who's going to sweep into your life and give you everything you want?'

God but he was cruel, she thought. 'Does he exist, Dirk? I doubt it. You were once my dream man. And look what happened—you turned out to be the devil in disguise.'

Laura's breath caught at the emotion that suddenly swirled into Dirk's eyes. They blazed for no more than a second or two, and what the emotion was, exactly, she couldn't grasp. Anger? Frustration? Surely not *distress*?

Whatever it was, it was gone before she could get a handle on it, to be replaced by an almost evil glitter that chilled her soul. 'The devil, eh? That gives me plenty of latitude, then. You won't be shocked by anything I suggest.'

Her stomach contracted. 'Nothing *you* would suggest would either shock or interest me.'

'That's not the impression I got the other night when you kissed me back so—er—enthusiastically.'

Laura could feel the dreaded heat gathering in her cheeks. 'I told you,' she spat under her breath, 'I'd been drinking. It didn't mean a thing.'

He leant over and picked up the bottle of wine, topping up her glass. 'Drink up, then. That way you can convince yourself afterwards it still doesn't mean a thing if we end up in bed together tonight.'

The sound that came from Laura's throat was weird, the result of trying to swallow a strangled gasp of outrage just before it burst from her lips. A volatile person in private, Laura hated scenes in public—hence her attempts to stifle her mixture of shock and furious indignation. She settled for a savage glare across the table at him.

'Before you tar and feather me with your eyes, Laura,' Dirk said drily, 'hear me out. You might find that what I have to suggest is both sensible and desirable for both of us.'

Laura scooped in then let out a long, shuddering breath.

'I take it your still remaining seated means you'll listen to my proposal?' he drawled.

'You can take it that I'm too damned flabber-gasted to move!'

'My, you *have* developed some extra fire this past year, haven't you? Not that you didn't always have a temper. But sexual frustration does become you, my darling. You look extraordinarily beautiful with that wild colour in your face and those angry lights in your eyes. I can see things could be even better the second time round.'

'I'm *not* your darling, and there certainly *won't* be a second time round!'

She went to stand up but his hand seized her wrist and he ground her back down into her seat. 'You forgot to deny the sexually frustrated part,' he rasped.

She glared at him, her mouth remaining tightly shut. But, inside, her mind was whirling, her heart pounding. She shouldn't have come here tonight. She had underestimated Dirk's physical power over her. For underneath her apparent protesting, her supposed indignation, she actually wanted to hear his disgusting proposal. That was why she'd tried to flee. She was running away from the shockingly excited anticipation that was firing her blood and making her want to forget how much this man had already hurt her.

'Now . . .' He released her hand and picked up his glass once more, draining it. 'Since you want to leave so desperately, what do you say I pay the bill and we go for a walk while I explain what I have in mind for us?'

Her panic surfaced in a brusque laugh. A cosy little walk along darkened city streets was infinitely more dangerous than remaining right where she was. 'No, thanks. It's drizzling, remember? Say what you have to say right here. And be quick. It's getting late and I'm tired.'

'You've turned into a hard woman, Laura,' he reprimanded quietly.

'And you've turned into an amoral bastard,' she returned equally quietly.

His shrug was casual. 'That all depends on the definition of amoral. And by what morals you're forming your judgement.'

She just shook her head, unable to believe this conversation. 'I used to think we shared the same sort of standards, Dirk,' she said shakily. 'But I was wrong. You have no real concept of right and wrong, have you?'

There was no doubt she had struck a nerve with this observation, for his mouth tightened briefly. But he quickly recovered, a small sardonic smile playing around his mouth. 'That's one of the problems with you, Laura. Your mother taught you to think in black and white concepts such as right and wrong, good and bad, love and hate. But there's a lot of grey between all those extremes. Maybe you'll realise that one day. As for myself, I assure you that as a lawyer who defends people every day I have a very accurate knowledge of right and wrong.'

'Only in a legal sense,' she snapped, angry that he'd criticised her mother. She might not have been perfect but she had done her best, and it couldn't have been easy bringing up a child alone after her so-called love had dumped her. 'In my opinion— and a lot of other people's too—there are no excuses for your disgusting behaviour lately.'

He laughed.

She stared at him, at the strong, classical lines that made up his handsome face, at his beautiful grey eyes, so bright and clear and intelligent, at that stubbornly square chin with the tiny cleft, and finally at the wide, well-shaped mouth that had spoken up for many a lost cause, but which was now pulled back with cynical amusement.

Suddenly, Laura was consumed by feelings of bewildering ambivalence—love and desire alongside dismay and a deeply disturbing frustration. She wanted her old Dirk back, not this wicked stranger.

Yet it was this wicked stranger she was wanting at this moment, this wicked stranger who was affecting her very badly indeed. The temptation to lean forward and press her lips to that laughing mouth was excruciatingly strong.

'Say what you have to say, for God's sake,' she rasped, shaken to the core by the depth of her desires.

The laughter left his face, and was replaced by a cold, cruel arrogance she found highly unnerving. Dirk had never been a man to be trifled with. But this new Dirk would make a formidable foe indeed.

'My proposal is simple, Laura,' he stated boldly. 'I want you to become my mistress.'

Laura stopped breathing.

'I realise that's a rather out-of-date term,' he went on as though he were discussing a shopping-list or something equally mundane. 'But it describes exactly the relationship I want to have with you. I'll pay all your bills, naturally. And give you lots of lovely expensive presents. In return for which I get unlimited and exclusive access to your body.'

His eyes darkened to slate as they slid down that body and up again. 'Well?' he said at last with a chilling little smile. 'What do you say?'

Laura felt the hysteria bubbling up inside her. I should be disgusted, she was thinking frantically. *Appalled*! And what am I feeling? Excited... aroused...

'*Unlimited and exclusive access to your body.*'

Oh, my God...

'You don't have to look so stunned, Laura,' he drawled. 'If you think about it, it's not such a shocking suggestion, and there are benefits on both sides. I get what I've always wanted from you with no emotional involvement. You, in turn, satisfy your own sexual needs, at the same time making yourself financially more secure for the future.'

He sighed when she remained silent and speechless.

'I see I must argue my case some more. First things first... We still fancy each other like mad. That's a fact you can't really deny, given your response to me the other night. Either that, or you're so damned frustrated, you're in need of a man post-haste! Since you admit you haven't found anyone else to sleep with, I'm sure I'd do as well, if not *better* than most.'

He leant back in his chair and surveyed her again with a lazy sensuality that had Laura's pulse-rate going right off the rails. She exhaled her long-held breath and forced herself to lean back as well, trying to look in control. But her hands were clenched so tightly around her serviette in her lap that they were in danger of going blue.

'For *my* part,' he went on smoothly, 'I admit that I've never found another woman who physically pleases me as much as you originally did. So why shouldn't we give ourselves mutual satisfaction and become lovers? What's to stop us? We won't be hurting anyone. Put aside your old-world, straitlaced ideas, my darling, and look reality in the face. Do you want to spend your nights alone and celibate while you wait for Mr Wonderful to show up? What if he never does?'

He cocked his head on one side and gave her one of his most charming, charismatic smiles. 'You're a beautiful woman, Laura, with a very beautiful body. It seems a shame to let it go to waste, don't you think?'

She didn't say a word. She merely dropped her serviette on the table, picked up her bag, stood up and left without a backward glance, her whole body trembling as she made her way carefully down the staircase and through the spacious foyer of the hotel. The taxis were queued up outside, and Laura was settled in one and speeding for home in no time.

Dirk Thornton remained at his table, twirling the empty glass in his hands, eyes narrowed, expression dark and pensive. When the waiter, Jonathan, approached and asked if he wanted another drink, he was given short shrift and the bill was demanded. Two minutes later, Laura's husband was striding away from the table, a preoccupied but harshly resolute look on his face, totally oblivious of the various lustful glances women threw after him.

CHAPTER FIVE

'AUNTY LAURA, Aunty Laura!' Donna chanted with delight. She was jumping up and down on the front porch in her nightwear, waiting for Laura to climb the steep path that wound from the street up to the house.

'Wow!' Laura puffed once she'd made it. 'What a climb! I'm glad I'm wearing a tracksuit and trainers. Still, it's no wonder your mummy is so lovely and slim if she does this every day.'

Carmel materialised at the open front door, busily putting earrings in. 'Who's calling who slim? If you turned sidewards I wouldn't see you these days, Laura. Aren't you eating properly?'

'Hey!' Laura laughed. 'I came over to baby-sit, not to get a dose of mothering. Of course I'm eating. How else would I have the strength to scale Mount Everest there?'

'Yes,' Carmel sighed. 'It *is* a trial, living on the side of a hill, but the view is worth it, don't you think?'

Laura turned to survey the panorama below of Manly Beach with its magnificent Norfolk pines lining the foreshore and the dark blue waves slapping lazily at the white sands.

'Without a doubt,' she agreed. 'And now, Miss Muffet,' she directed at Donna, 'I hope you've got plenty of games ready for us to play tonight? There's nothing worth seeing on television.'

Donna's eyes lit up. 'I'll go and get them all out right now!' she enthused, and raced inside.

'It's very good of you to do this for us on such short notice, Laura,' Carmel said warmly. 'I couldn't believe it when Kirsty rang to say she was sick and couldn't baby-sit tonight. I knew I'd have little hope of getting anyone else on a Saturday, and then—lo and behold!—the phone rang and it was you saying you wanted to come over this afternoon. I hope you don't think we had too much of a hide to ask you to mind the kids for us tonight instead?'

'Don't be silly! I was thrilled to be able to help out and see the kids at the same time.'

'I'll make it up to you next weekend and have a barbecue especially in your honour. That is, if you haven't anything else planned?'

'No. No plans as yet. I'll look forward to it.'

'You—er—weren't going out yourself this evening, were you? You didn't go putting off a date, did you?'

Laura thought she detected something in Carmel's question which suggested some secret knowledge. Or hope.

Understanding struck with a wry note. 'Ah...Morrie told you about catching me kissing Dirk last Saturday night, didn't he?'

It was perfectly clear immediately that he hadn't, and Laura bit her lip. Damn. Now I've let the cat out of the bag! she thought.

Carmel was looking at her with a mixture of shock and curiosity.

'It was nothing,' Laura dismissed. 'An aberration of the moment. Please forget it. Let's go inside.'

Carmel followed her avidly, unwilling to let the matter drop. 'But I *can't* forget it. I mean...you *kissed* him? After he—er—yes, well...'

Laura forged along the hallway into Carmel's huge combined kitchen and family room, where she levered herself up on to one of the stools fronting the breakfast-bar.

Carmel was hot on her heels. 'Still...it would be great if you and Dirk *did* get back together again. Just like old times! I mean...I know he's acted like a louse, but you and he seemed so right for each other, Laura. Everyone could see that. That's why we were all so surprised when you broke up.'

Laura faced her excited sister-in-law with a calm façade, though she was anything but calm inside. It was less than twenty-four hours since she'd walked out on Dirk in that restaurant, and inside she was still an emotional and physical mess.

'There is absolutely *no* chance of us getting together again, Carmel,' she stated firmly. 'I saw Dirk briefly last night and——'

'You did?' Carmel interrupted. 'Where?'

'Nowhere special. Some place in town.' No doubt the people who ran Kable's would cringe if they heard their establishment described thus, since it was touted as one of the best and most exclusive eating places in Sydney. But Laura would only ever remember it as the setting of one of the most humiliating moments of her life. Not only because Dirk had offered her the ultimate in degrading proposals, but because she'd been sorely tempted to accept.

Only momentarily, however, and only because her strength of purpose had been undermined by her own desires. Her relationship with Dirk had begun with great physical passion, and although the intensity had waned somewhat during their years of living together—probably because of her obsession with having a baby—their separation seemed to have brought this side of her feelings for him back with a vengeance. Being so close to him last night had been a trial and a torment. How she'd summoned the courage to walk away amazed her, when every part of her body was screaming to her to say yes, yes—to agree to *anything* to be in his arms once more!

Noticing that Carmel was still staring at her, waiting for more, Laura pulled herself together. 'I've asked Dirk for a divorce,' she stated coolly, 'and he was only too happy to start the proceedings. It's over. Our marriage is over. And you know what? I'm relieved. I finally realised that I don't love him any more after all.'

Bravo, a cynical little voice mocked at the back of her head. That's telling her! And what's a white lie here and there if it gets her off your back? Clever of you, however, not to mention that stunning little offer Dirk made you, or you might have confessed that it excited the hell out of you at the time and that you just managed to get away before you were on your knees in front of him!

Carmel's face had fallen. 'Oh, what a shame,' she murmured.

Shame...

That was indeed the operative word!

Laura's relief was enormous that she *had* found the strength to spurn Dirk's offer. How would she have felt today if she hadn't, if she'd let Dirk take her home to bed?

Certainly not as tense as you are at this moment, that wickedly insidious voice taunted.

'For pity's sake, it was inevitable,' she snapped, more at this dark inner voice than at Carmel herself. 'Sorry,' she apologised straight away. 'I'm still a bit touchy about Dirk, I suppose. Let's not talk about him any more. Now...tell me about this cocktail party you're off to. You said it's at some big-time theatrical producer's house and that he's coming to see the performance of *South Pacific* afterwards? It's the final show tonight, isn't it?'

'Yes and yes and yes!' Carmel grinned, easily distracted from any subject by talking about her husband. For a second, Laura was profoundly jealous. Carmel and Morrie had a great marriage and a great relationship, sharing everything together. Laura had once felt so secure seeing Dirk's brother in his role as husband and father. Like brother, like brother, she'd believed. How wrong could she have been?

Morrie walked into the kitchen just then, looking very spiffy in a black dinner suit, dress shirt and black bow-tie. A smaller package than Dirk, he was equally handsome and just as damned clever.

'What a life-saver you are, Laura!' he beamed, and gave her a kiss on the cheek before turning to his wife. 'Ready, honey? God, you look delicious. New dress?'

Carmel flushed with pleasure. She was a very pretty woman, and the slinky red gown she was wearing suited both her fair colouring and her shapely figure. The thought popped into Laura's mind that both brothers liked the same sort of dresses. Clingy. Revealing. And easily disposed of.

Morrie drew his wife into his arms for a rather long kiss which left Carmel quite flustered.

'For goodness' sake, Morrie,' she said, pushing him away with an embarrassed laugh. 'Whatever will Laura think?'

'That I won't be able to wait to get you home tonight,' he chuckled sexily.

This was the last kind of exchange Laura wanted to witness, for it reminded her too explicitly of Dirk and what he wanted of her. God, if only she were the sort of woman who could accept such an outrageous relationship. If only she could throw away all those obstructive ideals such as self-respect and decency, caring and commitment. If only she didn't *love* the bastard!

After they'd gone, Laura was infinitely glad of Donna's wish to play game after game. And Nicholas, for once, was an angel, though she kept him riveted to cartoon videos till it was time for bed. Unfortunately, that heralded the end of

Nicholas's co-operation. He whinged and grizzled during the entire proceedings. Even as she was tucking him into bed he was complaining.

'If you don't behave,' Laura warned, 'I'll call your Uncle Dirk and ask him to come over, and he'll be very cross.'

Laura blocked out any feeling of guilt at this suggestion. Nicholas was not to know that 'Uncle Dirk' was the last person on earth she'd ring up and ask to come over.

Nicholas looked suitably chastened. Dirk had once had to rescue him from a roof, necessitating a dangerous climb. He had given the little boy a bawling out afterwards that would have terrified a high-court judge.

'I'll be good,' the child said in a small voice.

'I'm glad to hear it,' Laura pronounced and, pecking him on the forehead, marched over to the door. 'Do you want me to leave the light on?'

'Course not!' he pouted. 'I'm not a scaredy-cat, like my stupid sister. I'm a big brave boy. I don't believe in boogie-men and monsters!'

Laura rolled her eyes in exasperation as she snapped off the light. But when she turned and saw Donna standing there, tears in her eyes, she wanted to go back inside and slap Nicholas.

'I...I can't help being s-scared, Aunty Laura. Sometimes I dr—dream about monsters and...and...if it's dark when I wake up, I...I think the monsters might be there hiding in my room.'

Laura resisted the temptation to pick Donna up and cuddle her. Sometimes sympathy like that was the worst thing one could offer. It set off the tears and self-pity all the more. Instead, she took Donna's hand and began to lead her slowly along the hallway.

'Do you really dream about monsters?' she said in an interested tone. 'I dream too, but I never dream about interesting things like monsters. My dreams are very boring. Maybe I should watch some more of those cartoons you and Nicholas watch and then I'll have exciting monster dreams too.'

She smiled down at Donna, who looked up with a surprised look in her eyes as though she'd never thought of her dreams as anything anyone would envy.

'Aren't you a lucky little girl,' Laura reinforced, 'to have such exciting dreams? Of course, dreams are just like cartoons on television. They can't hurt you, you know. They don't really exist. Someone makes them up and draws them on a computer. Once you turn off the television... Poof! The monsters are gone. Waking up does the same thing to dreams. Poof! They're gone.'

Again she smiled down at Donna, whose young mind seemed to be ticking over with astonishing new concepts, ones that obviously soothed her fears and boosted her self-esteem at the same time.

Laura felt very pleased with herself when Donna went to bed quite happily without the light on. However, she wasn't quite so smug ten minutes later when the little girl came screaming downstairs into the family-room.

'Aunty Laura, Aunty Laura! Nicholas is stuck and he can't get out and it's all my fault and...and...'

Laura tried not to panic, jumping up and taking Donna's small shaking shoulders within firm hands and saying, 'Calm down and tell me where Nick's stuck.'

'On top of the stairs!' the child cried. 'Come on, I'll show you.'

Laura was dragged down the hall and into the foyer.

'Up there!' Donna pointed.

Laura glanced up and saw a headful of blond curls sticking through the banister rails. A woebegone, tear-stained little face looked back down at her. 'Get me outa here!' Nicholas wailed.

'Oh, my God,' Laura groaned. 'Come on, Donna, we'll go and see what we can do.'

I could cheerfully kill that child, she thought mutinously as she made her way up the long curving staircase.

'How on earth can you say this was *your* fault, Donna? It's your *brother's* head wedged between these posts!'

'Well, he was calling me names through the wall and——'

'I wasn't!'

'You shut up, you little tyrant,' Laura said, giving him a poke in the bottom. 'Go on, Donna.'

'Well, when he wouldn't stop I told him I heard you ringing up someone, and said it was probably Uncle Dirk. He...he got out of bed and crept along the end of the hall and poked his head through so he could bend over and see the phone better, and got stuck and...I...I didn't mean him to get hurt!' she insisted. 'Honest. I just wanted him to stop calling me a scaredy-cat and a big baby for being 'fraid of the dark.'

'Get me outa here!' Nicholas screamed again, then burst into tears. The shoulder-shaking sobs softened Laura's heart, for he was, after all, only a little boy.

'Hush, darling,' she soothed, and bent down beside the distressed child. 'You'll be all right. Now try to stop crying and let Aunty Laura see what she can do. Donna, you run and get Nicholas some tissues.'

'But I'm weally st—stuck,' he sniffled.

'Yes ... you weally are,' she agreed with a hidden smile.

But she didn't smile for long. Nicholas's head and ears had swollen slightly with persistent tugging backwards, and she doubted he would ever get his head through the small gap. One of the posts would have to be cut away.

'I think we need help here,' she thought aloud.

'I want my mummy and daddy!' Nicholas sobbed.

Laura wiped his streaming nose with the tissues. 'So do I,' she muttered.

Morrie and Carmel had left telephone numbers in case of an emergency, but she was loath to drag them away from what might be the opportunity of a lifetime. After all, Nicholas's life was hardly threatened. No... a policeman was definitely the answer.

'You stay here and comfort your brother, Donna, while I telephone for help.'

Laura was hardly at the bottom of the stairs when the front doorbell rang.

'Well, heavens be praised!' she exclaimed, and raced to answer it, hoping that the caller was male and capable.

He was.

Unfortunately.

'Laura,' Dirk said lazily from where he was standing under the porch light. It gave her a splendid view of his impressive male body, rigged out to perfection in black trousers and white dinner-jacket, the same body she'd rejected less than twenty-four hours before.

Clearly, her rejection hadn't bothered Dirk unduly, since here he was, dressed in sartorial splendour, on his way out!

Laura wondered caustically which woman was to be the lucky recipient of his charms this evening. Virginia? Or some other equally rapacious creature?

'Visiting Carmel, are we?' he suggested, cool grey eyes raking over her casual attire.

'No,' came her short reply. 'Look, we don't have time for a deep and meaningful discussion on what vengeful God made you drop in here on the same night I was called upon to baby-sit.' And, ignoring the rampage of emotions that could have taken over if she let them, Laura grabbed Dirk's hand and dragged him inside.

He lurched in with raised eyebrows. 'There's no need for such indecent haste, Laura. If you've changed your mind about accepting my offer I would prefer to go about it with some style and——'

'Belt up and look up,' she commanded testily.

It was with a certain malicious pleasure that she watched his face change.

'That little bugger,' he said at last through gritted teeth.

'Tch, tch, tch,' she reprimanded drily. 'Not in front of the children.'

Laura took a backward step when he swung a decidedly sexual gaze her way. 'Whatever you say, darling. We'll wait till I have them safely tucked up in beddy-byes before we—er—proceed. *You* were the one who seemed over-anxious a moment ago.'

'Why, you——'

'Not in front of the children,' he broke in, placing a mocking finger over her angrily parted lips.

It was the wrong moment to close her mouth, with his finger pressed against her lips. The contact of flesh rubbing against sensitive flesh sent an electric shiver running through her. When she compounded the problem by gasping her lips back open, Dirk's left eyebrow lifted.

'Mmm,' he murmured, and actually went to put his finger inside her mouth.

She rocked backwards and struck his hand away. 'How dare you?' she spat.

His smile was the smile of the devil. 'Let me warn you,' he said with menacing softness, 'I dare to do a lot of things these days...

'And now,' he said more loudly, head tipping back to look up at Nicholas again, 'what have you done this time, my adventurous lad?'

It took them quite a while to free Nicholas, but in the end they didn't need to mangle the banister as Laura had feared. An ice-packed towel was placed around his head and neck for a good quarter of an hour, then his ears firmly stuck down against his head with masking tape. Loads of Vaseline applied to his head ensured that he virtually slid out when carefully eased backwards. The only danger was the amount of Vaseline left behind in Nicholas's hair which had to be thoroughly shampooed out before putting the exhausted little tyke to bed.

The only good thing to come out of the experience was a change in the relationship between brother and sister. A contrite Donna comforted and cosseted her baby brother during his ordeal like an old mother hen. Afterwards, he was definitely looking at her with different eyes. She was his guardian angel, his saviour, his other 'mummy', and he insisted she stay in the room with him and tell him a story, even though in no time he fell asleep.

When Donna finally climbed back into her own bed she was a different child—all puffed up and proud of herself.

'He *is* only little,' she told Laura. 'He doesn't mean to be naughty.'

'He needs someone to watch over him all the time,' Laura said ruefully.

'*I'll* do it.'

'Will you? Oh, what a good, kind sister you are. I wish I'd had a big sister like you.'

'Haven't you got a sister, Aunty Laura?'

'No. I haven't got a brother either. My mother only had the one baby and I have to say it was rather lonely growing up sometimes. It would have been nice to have a brother or sister to love.'

Donna's straight brown brows pulled together into a slight frown. 'When you have babies, Aunty Laura,' she said seriously, 'you'd better have more than one so they won't be lonely growing up.'

Laura's heart turned over and she couldn't bring herself to say a word. She just sat there on the side of the bed, staring blankly at Donna's wall and trying to get a hold of herself.

Donna's hand crept into hers. 'Don't be sad, Aunty Laura. *I* love you.'

Now a huge lump welled up in Laura's throat. 'And I love you,' she managed to get out in a strangled voice.

A sound behind them sent Laura's head whirling round to catch Dirk disappearing from the opened doorway, his strides sounding angry as he stalked off.

Her stomach twisted. Dirk had obviously overheard their conversation about having babies and reacted badly. Was this due to irritation? Or distress? Not for the first time she wondered if despair at his sterility could be responsible for the drastic change in his behaviour.

It was possible, she supposed. But unlikely. Laura couldn't bring herself to start hoping for near miracles. If Dirk wanted a child so desperately, he could have had one with her, by artificial insemination, or even adoption. But he hadn't even been prepared to talk about it.

No. He liked doing what he was doing, liked sleeping with any woman who took his fancy. And definitely liked shocking his stuffy, morally boring wife!

Maybe that was what was behind his outrageous proposal last Friday night. The wish to shock her, to exert some sort of revenge for the bruising she'd once given to his male ego. Hadn't she cruelly and stupidly said she didn't want him if he couldn't give her a baby? Well, he was probably out to prove that he could make her want him without offering her anything in exchange, except the ultimate insult. Cold hard cash!

Hardening her heart, Laura kissed Donna goodnight once again and left the room. After checking that Nicholas was fast asleep, she made her way slowly down the stairs, grimly resolved not to let Dirk get under her skin, and definitely not to let him touch her.

CHAPTER SIX

LAURA walked into the family-room and stopped dead. 'And what do you think you're doing?' she flung at Dirk, who was quite clearly taking off his dinner-jacket and bow-tie and draping them over one of the kitchen chairs.

He lifted an annoyingly bland face. 'Making myself at home, I think it's called.' He walked across to where the family-room opened into a large television viewing area and picked up the TV guide resting on the glass coffee-table. 'What's on the box tonight, I wonder? Ah, yes, an old favourite of mine—Alfred Hitchcock's *North by Northwest*. Remember we watched it together late one night, Laura? Years ago, it seems. All snuggled up on our sofa together.'

His chuckle was low and sexy. 'Well...we *almost* watched it. If I recall rightly, poor old Cary Grant was getting himself into an awful pickle and I was becoming suitably engrossed when you started to——'

'That's enough, Dirk!' she cut in furiously, her face flaming as the image of what she'd started to do jumped vividly into her mind.

His shrug was careless. 'If you insist. But I really thought I'd brought you beyond such hypocrisies, my darling. There's nothing shameful in what we

80

used to do together. We were man and wife, after all. Still are, in fact,' he finished, giving her a speculative look that sent a warning shiver up and down her spine.

Crossing her arms defensively, she gave him a savage glare in return. 'Something that time and a divorce will shortly remedy! Now... I suggest you put your tie and jacket on and go, Dirk. I'm sure Virginia, or whoever you are supposed to be taking out tonight, is anxiously waiting your arrival.'

'You seem very well informed about my lady-friends,' he drawled. 'Have you been checking up on me?'

'Hardly,' she scoffed. 'If you don't want every Tom, Dick and Harry to know who your current lover is then don't advertise your liaisons so publically. Or, alternatively, swear your secretary to a vow of silence!'

He smiled. 'Poor June... I couldn't do that to her. Her only fun in life is to gossip. So! I gather dear old Claudia is still trying to stick the knife in your back?'

'What do you think?'

'I think you should throw in that job of yours and start a fashion agency of your own. You'd be a brilliant success! You shouldn't be working for Fenwick Fashions, Laura. You should be working for yourself!'

Laura could not stop the flush of pleasure spreading through her. Whatever he'd become, Dirk still had the ability to compliment her where it mattered most. Not on her looks, but on her achievements, both real and possible. It had been on his encouragement alone that she had applied for the fashion buying traineeship she'd seen in the paper one Saturday, eighteen months after her marriage. Her mother had thought her totally unsuited to a job that involved dealing with people on a business level and making important buying decisions. And she herself—after her miserable experiences at school—had been faint-hearted at her prospects of ever being anything above a shop assistant.

But she had taken to the job like a duck to water, her own natural fashion sense combining well with an earnest desire to prove herself as smart as her husband seemed to think she was. It had been extremely satisfying to see Dirk's pride in her success.

But even *he* was overestimating her this time.

'I don't think I have enough experience to strike out on my own,' she said hesitantly. 'Besides, I would need quite a bit of backing capital to start up a business. I...I don't have that kind of money, Dirk.'

'I'll give you as much money as you need,' he returned smoothly, 'if you agree to the proposal I made last night.'

Suddenly, Laura realised where his sneaky compliments and suggestions had been leading: right back into his sexual trap. It brought a bitter taste to her mouth and a flustered anger to her tongue. 'You have about as much chance of that happening as...as...'

'As I have of making love to you here tonight on this sofa?'

Laura gasped, then rallied to stride over and pick up his jacket and tie, throwing them at him. 'Get out of here. Right now!'

He merely caught the clothes and tossed them on to a nearby armchair, his attitude and expression one of amused indulgence. 'You don't have to get your knickers in a knot, Laura, honey. I can take a hint. So the answer's still no. Fine. But I'm not leaving. I've nowhere to go at the moment except home to an empty flat. I rang Virginia while you were washing Nicholas's hair and called off our date.'

'Just like that? No explanations or apologies?'

'Don't tell me you're worried about *Virginia's* feelings? Now that would be a first—the wife concerned about the other woman. But, if you must know, I did mention something about a family crisis. Unfortunately, Virginia leapt to the correct conclusion that *you* might be somehow involved and slammed the phone down in my ear.' His sigh was a complete mockery of concern. 'I'm going to have to work damned hard to get back into her good books after this.'

'I'm sure you'll find a way,' Laura snapped.

'True,' came his laconic and unabashed agreement.

For a second Laura thought she was going to explode with fury and frustration. Just in time, she gathered herself, knowing that to show Dirk any weakness was always a big mistake. A cool head was required to outmanoeuvre such a conniving devil, for clearly his insistence on staying meant he hadn't given up the idea of making her his mistress. She had not been fooled by his display of mild-mannered acquiescence in that regard. Not in the slightest.

'I really have no interest in discussing your powers of persuasion,' she said archly. 'Neither do I want the dubious pleasure of your company for the rest of the evening. So, if you don't mind, I'd still like you to leave.'

'How ungrateful of you, Laura! I come in and rescue that little tyrant for you, and what do I get in reward? Nothing but insults. Not even the offer of a cup of coffee.'

Laura let out a weary sigh. 'If I get you a cup, will you leave then?'

'You have my word.'

Which had become about as reliable as a politician's, she thought irritably.

Her qualms increased when Dirk picked up the remote-control on the TV then proceeded to stretch out on the deeply cushioned floral sofa.

One second later the images of Cary Grant and Eva Marie Saint filled the screen, unfortunately in a close clinch. Laura spun away and marched over to the galley-style kitchen, snapping on the kettle and rattling drawers as she prepared the coffee.

'Don't forget to make yourself a cup,' he called out. 'I hate drinking alone.'

'Tough,' she muttered under her breath.

'What was that?' He levered himself up far enough to peer over the back of the sofa at her.

'Just watch the film, Dirk, and shut up.'

'My, you're touchy this evening. Or are you touchy every evening? You know, what you need, Laura, is a good...long——'

'Dirk Thornton, if you say another word of that ilk I'm going to come over there and tip scalding coffee right over your you-know-what!'

His chuckle carried no remorse. 'I was only going to say holiday.'

'Like hell you were!'

'Laura, I'm shocked.'

'Pooh, you are!'

'Now who's using rude words?'

'Not me. I *never* swear.'

'You do too.'

'I do not!'

'You called me a bastard last night.'

'That's not swearing. That's just stating a fact,' insisted Laura.

'An opinion, not a fact. Factually, I'm not a bastard. Mum and Dad were quite definitely married by the time I came along.'

Laura gulped in a deep breath of air and was about to launch back with another caustic retort when she pulled herself up sharp.

You're enjoying this, she realised. Your heart's beating faster. Your blood's heating up. And your stupid damned body's only one level short of sexual arousal.

Soon, you won't want him to go at all. And you *know* where that might lead.

Yes, she thought breathlessly.

She glanced over at Dirk just as he sat up and twisted round to see what she was doing. Whatever he saw in her face made the laughter die in his eyes, to be replaced by a wicked knowingness that worried and annoyed her.

I've gone and done it again, she groaned silently. Betrayed my innermost feelings, let him know that underneath all my holier-than-thou protestings I still want him.

In quiet desperation Laura dropped her eyes and tried to will her pulse back to normal, all the time reminding herself of the resolves she'd made when she first came downstairs. Renewing her determination to treat him with the contempt he deserved, she carried the coffee over, placing the cup and saucer on the side-table next to him before retreating to an adjacent armchair. Sinking into its soft depths, she leant back and casually crossed her ankles, hoping she was giving a good display of cool indifference to his continuing presence. She even pretended to be watching the movie.

'Ah, no one makes a cup of coffee like you, Laura,' he praised after several sips. 'Hot and strong and sweet . . .'

Laura stiffened as she waited for him to add, Just like you. He'd made the comparison once while they were making love on their honeymoon, and for several months afterwards the act of drinking coffee together had taken on an intimacy something like foreplay. Dirk would deliberately catch her eye over the rim of his cup and mouth the words, and she would inevitably blush. He had seemed to like making her blush back in those days.

Of course . . . just like everything else in their relationship, the blushes had finally ceased, and drinking coffee no longer represented anything special.

Now, however, she could feel the heat zooming back into her cheeks. Pricked by a dreadfully self-conscious embarrassment, she darted a quick glance his way to see if he'd noticed her discomfort.

What a silly thing to do!

Those expressive grey eyes locked immediately with hers, telling her that he too had been remembering their coffee days—with great pleasure, judging by the smouldering lights glittering in his gaze.

Her heart leapt, but she reefed her own eyes away, all the while trying desperately to recapture her coolly indifferent air.

Dirk was not about to let her get away with things that easily.

'Can you give me a good reason,' he asked with insidious softness, 'why you won't become my mistress? No histrionics now. I'm not going to try to force the issue. I just want to know your objections, voiced calmly and logically.'

Laura swallowed convulsively. Could she risk answering his question, and thus inviting cross-examination? Dirk was the king of debate, of verbal arguings, of persuading people to his point of view. Dared she lock horns with him?

Probably not. But suddenly—maybe because it piqued her to be thought weak and susceptible— she wanted to show him she'd become a much stronger, more independent woman since he'd left her, and was not about to be talked into anything against her will, especially his outrageous proposal! As if she'd just let him use her like that anyway, after all he'd done. Good grief! The man must be mad!

'I can give you a whole host of reasons, Dirk, but the main three would be that first...I don't like you any more. Secondly...I just don't want to. And thirdly, I find your proposal disgustingly offensive.'

'Hmm.' He put the cup back on its saucer. 'You know, Laura, there was a time when you didn't find my making love to you disgustingly offensive. Just the opposite, in fact.'

'I didn't say your lovemaking was disgustingly offensive,' she corrected curtly. 'I said your *proposal* was. Being a man's paid mistress is tantamount to prostitution, in my view.'

'Oh, I see,' he nodded sagely. 'Then it's the *money* that offends you. Fair enough. I take back the offer of money and change my proposal from mistress to lover. Or do you prefer girlfriend?'

'I prefer ex-wife,' she said coldly. 'You seem to be conveniently forgetting my first two reasons.'

'No. I haven't forgotten. Firstly, you don't like me... Well, what's liking between lovers? A moot point. There's quite a few things about *you* I don't like but I'm quite prepared to overlook them.'

Laura sucked in a startled breath. 'Such as what?'

'You're horribly untidy for one thing. You leave the lids off everything in the bathroom and your idea of cleaning up is to throw everything in the bottom of your wardrobe. I bet if I went into your bedroom right now it would be a disaster!'

Laura coloured guiltily as she pictured her bedroom back at the unit. He was right. It was a mess. Not that it was totally her fault. It was partly *his*! She'd deliberately involved herself earlier today in making a new dress, sewing being an activity that required her total concentration. Housework would never have distracted her from thinking about Dirk and his evilly corrupting proposal. Then after lunch she'd rung Carmel, thinking she would visit her on Sunday, only to be suddenly landed with this baby-sitting job. There'd been no time for cleaning up!

'That's beside the point,' she dismissed with an irritable wave of her hand. 'You've forgotten the most important reason. I don't *want* you to make love to me.'

'You'd prefer to make love to *me*?' he shot back, wicked lights dancing in his eyes.

'Nice try, Dirk,' she said with suitable sarcasm, while inside battling to stop her blood overheating at the images his counter-suggestion evoked. It had been such a long time since she'd taken the aggressive role in making love to Dirk, since she'd let her hands and mouth speak her desires, since she'd been the one to make the running and control the outcome. Hell, it had been a long time since she'd made love in *any* way, shape or form—something her body was screaming out at her right now.

Just thinking about what she'd once been able to do to the man sitting next to her was sending shards of excitement quivering all through her veins. What would it be like to do it again, to make him groan with frustration, moan with pleasure, to send him way way out of control? She knew his body so well, knew what he liked, knew what would spin him into a vortex of passion from which there was only one escape.

'I can see I'm wasting my time,' Dirk pronounced at this ambivalent moment. Jumping to his feet, he swept the coffee-cup up to his lips only to spill the last of it down the front of his shirt. 'Damn and blast,' he muttered. 'This is my favourite shirt.' And without further ado he put down the cup and began undoing his cuff buttons.

For a few seconds, Laura just sat where she was, quite taken aback, especially by Dirk's uncharacteristic clumsiness. When she noticed that his fingers were actually shaking as he undid the buttons on his shirt, a startling thought crossed her mind. Could he be genuinely upset by her rejection? Was he, perhaps, still in love with her on some strange level?

Once again, she was bombarded with the whys and wherefores of her husband's seemingly complete reversal of character this past year, from a faithful loving mate to a wild carouser. *Was* his sterility at the base of all his outrageous behaviour?

What was the truth and what wasn't? Had he been lying when he claimed recently to have only married her out of lust? Could he have really been in love all along?

Yes, she decided with a rush of shaky emotion. Yes! She couldn't have been wrong about that. He *had* loved her.

Once...

Maybe she hadn't totally destroyed that love with her baby obsession. Maybe she'd only damaged it. Or maybe something had twisted inside of him when he'd found out he couldn't father a child—something that time and her love for him could cure...

Laura's head began to whirl with a baffling assortment of maybes and might bes. But then common sense came to her rescue. She couldn't be sure of anything, could she? She was only hypothesising, her own love for Dirk trying to find excuses for his highly unacceptable behaviour.

'I'll just go and soak this in the laundry tub,' he said, and stripped the shirt back off his shoulders.

Laura flinched. Did he have to take the darned thing right off in front of her? Right *now*?

It seemed he did.

Laura swallowed then did her best to look nonchalant while her eyes feasted on the well-honed flesh of Dirk's bare torso. There was no doubt he *had* been working out more often in the gym. Her hands curled over the edges of the arm-rests in defence of the urge to reach out and touch him, her breathing suspended till he turned and strode off.

Once he was safely gone she let the air escape from her lungs on a long, shuddering hiss. She slumped back in the chair, feeling exhausted.

The tap started running in the laundry-room, with Laura remaining grateful for the respite from Dirk's highly disturbing presence. But the sounds of water and washing were soon followed by the thrum of the drier, which was not so comforting. If Dirk meant to wait till his shirt was dry, then he would be around a good while longer.

Her response was a return to tension, accompanied by a small amount of panic. She didn't like the way things were going, especially within her own mind. Being with Dirk was bad enough. Being with a semi-naked Dirk was sheer torture!

When he finally returned, Laura was relieved to see he'd found a shirt of Morrie's to put on. Unfortunately, it was too small and the buttons had been left undone. The sides flapped open when he walked, movement rippling the muscles in the hard walls of his chest.

Laura's lips were dry by the time he sat down, and her heart was thudding in her chest, both reactions annoying her considerably. She didn't want to desire Dirk, and she certainly didn't want him to notice any agitation on her part. He had the nature of a vulture when it came to showing weaknesses.

'You could do with some sun,' came her sharp comment, born from a perverse compulsion to find something to criticise him over. Not that he was all that pale. Even during the cooler months, Dirk's normally bronzed skin always retained an attractive golden hue. His colouring was an unusual combination with his silvery blond hair and olive skin. Morrie was fair-haired too, but his skin didn't tan like Dirk's.

His shrug was indifferent as he stretched his arms along the back of the sofa. 'I haven't had much time for leisure lately. I've had one difficult case after another.'

'Either that, or your leisure hours are always spent indoors!'

This barbed remark brought a sardonic smile, and Laura could have kicked herself. 'Is that jealousy I hear? Or just sour grapes?' he asked.

'I'd call it disappointment and disgust!'

'Really? Is it my having sex you object to or my choice of partners?'

'Maybe it's the *number* of your partners! Don't you ever think about catching diseases, Dirk? Or do you like flirting with death?'

His dark frown surprised her. Surely a man as intelligent as himself had thought about such things? Though, to be honest, it was the first time *she* had. Her reactions to her husband's womanising had all been emotional, so far, rather than practical. Now, she was seized by a very real concern for his health. If anything horrible happened to Dirk, she would just die.

The fierceness of her distress sent her leaning forward on the chair towards him. 'Dirk, you...you aren't taking any silly chances, are you?' she said with genuine feeling. 'I mean...'

He too snapped forward, bringing his face quite close to hers. 'Do you honestly think I would ask you to be my mistress if there was any chance sleeping with me would bring you physical harm? You might not believe me, Laura, but I still care about you and would never risk your health. *Never!*'

She did believe him. Maybe she was foolishly naïve to do so, but she did. In fact she was incredibly moved by the depth of emotion that had vibrated in his voice with his assurances. It reminded her of the Dirk she had first met, the committed, passionate lawyer who had captivated her imagination and her heart, who had married her and shown her that a man could give a woman so much more than she had ever hoped for. It reminded her of the man she had first fallen in love with.

'Oh, Dirk,' she cried softly, and dropped her eyes in confusion at the feelings rushing through her.

'Laura . . . my love . . .'

When his right hand lifted to lie gently against her cheek, she looked up, her heart turning over when she saw the warmth and passion in his gaze. He still loved her. He *must*.

His first kiss was incredibly soft, his lips fanning lightly over her. She sighed when his mouth lifted.

His second kiss was not quite so innocent, his tongue demanding entrance into her mouth and his hand moving down to cup her throat with possessive strength. There was a split second of automatic resistance before Laura's lips parted, but it was quickly obliterated by an explosion of desire within her that was both devastating and self-destructive. For it carried no conscience, no thought of consequences, only an obsessive drive to have its deep needs totally satisfied.

She moaned when he eventually pulled back, her eyes fluttering open to stare over at him pleadingly.

'If we keep this up,' he rasped, 'I won't be able to stop. Tell me, are you sleeping here the night or will you be going home later?'

'I . . . I'm sleeping here.'

'Pity. Still, I suppose this will keep, since you've decided to stop all your jealous wife nonsense and act like the highly sexed woman you really are. Now don't go mouthing further self-righteous protests at me, Laura,' he growled, gripping her shoulders and literally dragging her out of her chair and on to his lap. 'You obviously need a man in your bed and it might as well be your husband!'

With that, he gathered her close and covered her mouth once more, forcibly reminding her that her flesh was far stronger than her weak-willed conscience, especially when aroused. And she *was* aroused. Stunningly so. Good God, she could actually feel the liquid heat between her thighs, feel the way her insides were twisting into a knot of tension only this man could calm.

She gave a whimpering groan of dismay when, once again, he abandoned her, this time depositing her firmly on to the sofa next to him. Surely he couldn't mean to leave her like this, she thought dazedly.

'Dirk,' she choked out, and without thinking slid her hands inside the open shirt and over his chest, pushing the garment aside. Bending forward, she pressed her lips to the hot, satiny flesh of one shoulder, trailing her mouth downwards till it grazed over the hard nub of a male nipple.

His moan told her all she needed to know and she kept going, down his chest, over his ribs, till she reached his navel. Her tongue-tip flicked out to run erotic circles around it, making his stomach muscles tighten and his breathing grow fast and shallow. But when her hands went to undo his trousers they were suddenly clasped in an iron grip.

'Don't, for God's sake,' he commanded huskily.

She lifted glazed eyes. 'Why not? Don't you like that any more?'

His laugh was strangled. 'Of course I do.'

'Then let me,' she whispered thickly. 'I want to.' And she leant forward to kiss his mouth while she reached again for the zip.

With an abruptness that left her gasping he pushed her away again and stood up. 'I said no, Laura,' he pronounced in an amazingly cold voice.

She gaped up at him.

'I'm sorry, but the truth is I've made other plans for later tonight. I had no idea you'd be so...co-operative. But don't worry, I'll make sure this is my swan-song with Virginia. As from tomorrow, I'm all yours. Salaam, my sweet,' he smiled, giving her the Arab salute of farewell. 'Sleep well and put all that lovely mad passion on hold for another twenty-four hours. I can see it will be worth waiting for. Don't get up. I'll let myself out.'

Laura still hadn't found her voice by the time she heard the front door bang shut. Gradually, all her senses returned, even if her brain-power was the slowest to resume operation. When it did, she groaned aloud in bitter anguish.

How could she *ever* have deluded herself into thinking he still cared for her? *How?* And to have abased herself so thoroughly by practically begging him to let her do what she had always considered the ultimate intimacy in love-play? She must have been insane!

A shamed heat burnt in her cheeks at how close she had come to total humiliation. Bad enough that he was going from kissing her to another woman's body. But what if she had actually...?

A deep shudder reverberated through her.

And then to have let him leave without telling him to go to hell, without correcting his assumption that she was prepared to...to...

'Oh, dear heaven,' she cried brokenly, and slumped sideways on the sofa. 'Whatever am I going to do?'

CHAPTER SEVEN

'You didn't have to wait up for us,' Carmel said when she and Morrie came home around one a.m.

'I thought I'd better,' was Laura's careful reply. No point in saying she had as much chance of sleeping as running for Prime Minister.

Despite feeling that she was closer to hating Dirk than ever before, her mind kept being haunted with visions of him and Virginia writhing naked together in some bedroom. Not a normal bedroom, either. An intensely decadent boudoir with red velvet wallpaper, indecently plush white carpet, a mirrored ceiling, and a huge circular bed with black satin sheets.

Intuitive Morrie was the first to react to her unspoken tension. 'Did something happen while we were out?' he asked.

Laura dragged her thoughts away from Dirk and Virginia and concentrated on Morrie, who was looking at her with speculative interest.

'Nothing drastic. There was a minor drama with Nicholas which I thought you should know about before the kids attempt a muddled version in the morning.'

Morrie frowned but Carmel sighed. 'What did he do *this* time?' she said wearily. 'No, wait! Let me get us a glass of port first. I think I could do with one before hearing of our son's latest exploits. What about you, Morrie? Laura?'

They both agreed to the port, Laura mentally reminding herself not to have more than one small glass. She had just decided what she was going to do about Dirk and it required her being fit to drive.

Once the three of them were settled in the family room with their nightcaps, Laura launched into the evening's events, including Dirk's part, except she made it sound as if he left immediately after the crisis was averted.

Carmel was shaking her head by the time the tale came to an end.

'I never know what to expect next from that little devil,' she complained. 'Truly, Morrie, you'll have to take a firmer hand with Nicholas.'

'I do my best, honey. He's a difficult child. Once he goes to school, he'll probably quieten down.'

'I think tonight's experience was a good lesson learnt,' Laura put in. 'He was very subdued afterwards. Dirk said there's nothing like some genuine fear and panic to dampen a rebellious spirit.'

'That was a stroke of luck, Dirk turning up like that,' Carmel remarked, a frown on her face. 'Did he say why he called round? I mean ... he knew we were going out. I heard Morrie tell him on the phone earlier in the afternoon.'

Laura shrugged. 'He didn't say. I guess the emergency distracted him from the purpose of his visit.'

'Or he came specifically to see you,' Carmel concluded. 'Though how he knew that you ...' She swung exasperated eyes towards her husband. 'Morrie, you didn't tell Dirk Laura was baby-sitting the kids, did you?'

There was no doubting the guilt in Morrie's face. 'I might have mentioned it in passing. Look, why the accusing tone? He's her husband, for heaven's sake. Maybe he just wanted to talk to her about something. Dirk didn't do anything to upset you, did he, Laura?'

'Just *seeing* Dirk upsets Laura,' Carmel went on irritably. 'As for him being her husband... Huh! That's something he conveniently forgot when he walked out on his marriage and started competing for the Stud-of-the-Century award!'

'Stop it!' Laura snapped, and leapt to her feet. 'Just stop it!'

Both Carmel and Morrie stared up at her with stricken faces.

'Please,' she cried. 'Don't start arguing with each other over Dirk and I. It... it makes me feel awful. You're the most genuinely happy couple I've ever known and I don't want...I...I...'

Tears welled up in her eyes.

Carmel was up and hugging her in one second flat. 'Oh, my poor darling,' she soothed. 'I'm so sorry. I'm a thoughtless idiot.'

Laura drew back, gulping hard. She knew if she started *really* crying, she wouldn't stop. And Dirk wasn't worth such tears.

She tried a laugh, but it came out shaky. 'They say a divorce is worse than a death in the family. I'm beginning to believe it.'

'A *divorce*?' Morrie exclaimed. 'But I thought...
I mean ... When did this happen?'

'Laura decided last week,' Carmel told him.

'But——'

'Look, she can't remain in limbo forever, Morrie.
Much as we love her and want her to stay our sister-
in-law, she has to think about the future. Laura's
given Dirk plenty of time to come to his senses and
try for a reconciliation, and now he's missed the
boat, hasn't he, love?'

'Yes,' she said, thinking bitterly that he might
have missed the boat but he had plenty of sleek
racing craft to fall back on.

'Dirk is *not* a bad man,' his brother defended
staunchly. 'He's just been troubled by something
lately. I...I think Laura should give him some more
time before taking such a final step as divorce. I
mean ... it's not as though she's met someone else
and wants to remarry!'

Laura was startled by the certainty behind this
last statement of Morrie's. How, she puzzled, could
he be so sure? He hadn't been privy to any details
of her private life over the last few months. Sure,
she saw him nearly every week at the theatre group
meetings, but, true to form, she wasn't one to
gossip, either about herself or others. He would
have no real idea if there was another man on her
scene or not.

Which meant he must have been talking about
her with Dirk.

She stared at her brother-in-law and worried over
just what part he was playing in Dirk's blatant at-

tempts to get her back into his bed. Was he a willing accomplice, or an unwitting one? It crossed her mind that it had been Morrie who had sent Dirk tickets for *South Pacific*. He could easily have made sure his brother's seats were right behind Laura's.

Anger and disappointment showed in her face.

'Don't look at me like that, Laura,' he groaned. 'He's my brother, for pity's sake. And you're the best thing that ever happened to him. Hell, you've no idea what he was like before he met you. The things he used to do! And no, I don't mean women, I mean the mad chances he used to take, defending all sorts of crazy criminal types no other lawyer would touch with a barge-pole! As a teenager, he was an incorrigible dare-devil. As a grown man, he wasn't much better, always going out on a limb, never counting the costs. If he thought someone was innocent, he adopted a no-holds-barred approach, regardless of the danger. But then he met you... and overnight he seemed to change into a steadier, much more sensible person. I began to think he might even *live* to be thirty-five. OK, so he seems to have gone off the rails at the moment. But is it too much to ask you to hang on a little longer? Don't give up on him yet, Laura. I'm begging you.'

Laura was moved by his brotherly-love plea. But it was clear Morrie knew nothing of Dirk's sterility problem, nor of his earlier admission that he had married her for lust alone, not love. And it was lust again prompting this renewal of interest in her.

Morrie mistakenly saw his brother's behaviour as a temporary aberration, not a lasting condition.

She knew better. Dick had proved to her once more tonight that he was a conscienceless devil. Her only surprise was his reluctance to bed both her and Virginia in the one night. Perhaps, at thirty-four, he felt himself physically incapable of such stamina. His reasons certainly couldn't be *moral* ones. A moral man did not flaunt other women in his wife's face, nor try to exploit what he knew his wife still felt for him.

For that was what he'd been trying to do. Use her love to selfishly take for himself the only part of her he still wanted: her body.

Her heart turned over with dismay when she saw Morrie's distressed face. She wanted to reassure him, wanted to say that she still loved Dirk, and would not abandon him, despite everything.

But she couldn't do it. Love wasn't indestructible, and hers for Dirk had finally begun to crumble.

Oh, yes, no doubt he could still affect her sexually. That would perhaps take a long time to die, since sexual attraction was not subject to reason. But she could no longer keep loving a man she neither liked, nor respected.

'Dirk has made his bed, Morrie,' she said in a regretful but rueful tone. 'I'm afraid he must lie in it.'

'But Laura, he——' He broke off, a grimace twisting his mouth. Laura got the impression he wanted to say more, but wasn't sure he should.

'Yes?' she prompted.

He sucked in then expelled a shuddering sigh. 'Dirk is a very complex man. Sometimes, his approach to life's problems is . . . unorthodox. But I repeat . . . he's *not* a bad man. Always remember that.'

Laura tried not to show pity on her face. Morrie just didn't know his brother as well as he thought he did. That was the problem. But she couldn't bring herself to disillusion him.

She patted him soothingly on the shoulder. 'Whatever you say, Morrie. Now I must be going.'

Carmel stared at her. '*Going*? At *this* hour? I thought you were staying the night.'

'Sorry, but I'm a hopeless sleeper in a strange bed, especially when I'm wound up like this.'

'Dirk *did* upset you, didn't he?'

Laura neither confirmed nor denied Carmel's comment.

Carmel looked beseechingly at her husband, but he merely shrugged. 'I'll walk you down to your car,' he offered, and Laura nodded.

It was after two by the time Laura parked her red Laser in her garage. Her hand trembled as she reached to turn off the ignition, only then realising that she couldn't remember the drive home at all. Just as well there wasn't much traffic on the road at that time of morning.

Her mind had been on Dirk, of course, but, strangely enough, her thoughts had been sad rather than angry and bitter.

She could understand Morrie's frustration, for she too wanted to believe that Dirk was basically a good man. But it just wasn't so. As they said in the classics, actions spoke louder than words and, quite frankly, his actions of late would have done the Marquis de Sade proud. Fancy blithely going from her arms to another woman's bed, all the while telling her it would be *her* bed he graced the next night!

Laura climbed out of the car and slammed the door.

The trouble was, she thought bleakly as she pulled the garage door down, Dirk could probably achieve his aim, if her sexual responses to him tonight were anything to go by. No doubt his intention was to show up at their unit tomorrow— make that today, she amended as she realised the time—looking dashingly handsome and extraordinarily sexy, then proceed to take up where he thought Laura had left off.

Taking a deep, steadying breath, she inserted her key in the stairwell security door, blocking out any memory of how well Dirk could make love when he set his mind to it. How…imaginative…he could be.

She focused her mind on the course of action she'd decided to take to avoid the catastrophe of her husband seducing her against her better judgement.

Laura reached the first floor of the three-storeyed block of units, checked that the hallway was empty—no lurking husbands around—then walked swiftly along to her door. In seconds she was safely inside, deadlocks and door-chain in place.

She leant against the door and emitted a ragged sigh. By eight o'clock—less than five hours away—she was planning on being back in her car and spending the day as far away from this unit as she possibly could, returning late in the evening. Patience was not one of Dirk's virtues, and he would get extremely tired of waiting for her to answer her phone or the door. In the end—hopefully before she came home—he would give up and go home to his bachelor pad.

Of course that would only solve her problem for one day. But one day was a start, and hopefully Dirk would soon get the message that he was wasting his time with her.

Laura levered herself away from the door and strode into the main bedroom, her resolve as purposeful as her walk. Only one thing puzzled her. Did Dirk honestly imagine that she would stay at home all day waiting for him to arrive, then meekly succumb to his sexual demands? The man must indeed be mad! Whatever, he needed someone to show him that he couldn't get away with treating women like erotic toys, to be picked up and discarded at whim.

'And I'm voting myself chief shower-upperer!' she pronounced aloud, angrily tossing her holdall on to the bed she'd once shared with Dirk.

It bounced then landed on the pillow where Dirk's head had once rested. Laura glared at the pillow, then at the entire right side of the bed, the side which Dirk had always claimed was the only side he could sleep on.

'Which was probably another damned lie,' she muttered crossly.

But she had laughed at him when he'd first made the claim, on the night they'd returned from their honeymoon.

Laura sank down on the side of the bed, her anger pushed aside as the memories crowded in, memories of a time when their future had looked rosy, when Dirk had seemed to answer *all* her needs, not just her sexual ones, when nothing and no one could have shaken her faith in his love.

'But why must you sleep on that side?' she'd queried, her smile indulgent. 'You certainly didn't always sleep on the same side every night during our honeymoon.'

He'd grinned at her across the bed. Both of them had their suitcases resting on the quilt and were in the process of unpacking. 'I don't seem to recall sleeping those nights at all.'

'But you're going to from now on?' she teased.

'Unfortunately. It's back to work tomorrow for both of us. Back to reality.'

'Reality,' she repeated slowly, a cloud settling around her heart.

Seeing her change of mood, Dirk had walked around the foot of the bed to draw her into his arms. His kiss was tender, his embrace reassuring. 'Don't be sad,' he said softly. 'Honeymoons can't go on forever. Reality always returns. But reality with you, my darling, will be more wonderful than a million honeymoons with any other woman. You're all I could ever want in a wife.'

'Am I, Dirk?' she asked, some well-hidden doubts spilling out all of a sudden. 'Am I really?' She couldn't help remembering what her mother had cruelly told her the day before their wedding—that the marriage couldn't possibly last, that even if Dirk had fallen in love with her she just didn't have what it took to keep a man like him.

His hands had cupped her face. 'What can I say to convince you? I adore you, Mrs Laura Thornton. Simply adore you.'

'But... but I'm not very smart, you know. Not like you are.'

He'd laughed incredulously at that. 'Not smart? Why, you're the smartest little miss on two legs! You caught me, didn't you, the most determined bachelor in Sydney? Caught me, threw me and hog-tied me with just one look from those beautiful blue eyes of yours.'

'But that's not——'

'Now hush up,' he'd cut in firmly. 'I don't want to hear any more of that. You're very smart and don't let anyone tell you differently. You just haven't received the right encouragement.'

He'd kissed her then, not so gently this time. A minute or two later, their two suitcases had been pushed off on to the floor with Dirk demonstrating that he was equally efficient on either side of their marital bed.

Laura clasped her hands to the sides of her head and moaned softly, not so much in longing for

Dirk's lovemaking, but for the Dirk she'd first married. It was so hard to believe that *that* Dirk was merely an illusion, that he'd been playing a role simply to possess her in a sexual sense. She desperately wanted to believe that he had really loved her back then; that the man she'd crossed swords with tonight was a wicked aberration, twisted by the knowledge of his sterility, warped by his seemingly futile future.

Morrie was obviously hoping that the changes in his brother's character were only temporary. Laura could not afford to start grasping at such a straw, for there was no evidence that this could be true. Dirk's behaviour, if anything, was becoming more and more outrageous.

Thinking once again about his parting words tonight resurrected Laura's outrage and anger. If Dirk thought he could worm his way back into her bed as easily as that he had another think coming! She was no longer the naïve teenager he had first met. She was a confident woman now. A survivor of the first order.

Laura jumped to her feet, her chin up, her resolve strong. Let him try to seduce her. Let him just try!

CHAPTER EIGHT

SUNDAY dawned blessedly fine, with the promise of a warm autumn day. Laura was on the road shortly after eight, heading for one of the beaches on the southern side of Sydney, far away from Dirk. Cronulla would do, she decided on the spur of the moment when she spotted a sign shortly after negotiating the Harbour Bridge.

Not that she intended swimming. The water would be far too cold. A nap while lying in some warm sand wouldn't go astray, however, she thought, a yawn capturing her mouth for the umpteenth time.

And sleep in the sand she did. All morning. Mental and physical exhaustion had finally taken its toll. Afterwards, she walked. Up and down the beach. Up and down. Finally she sat, and with the sitting came the worrying thoughts. Would Dirk really give up waiting for her to come home and meekly go away?

He'd never given up on anything in his life, Laura knew. He hadn't let her give up on anything either. At his instigation and with his help she'd learnt to swim, learnt to read better, learnt to drive. She'd even got a better job. He'd driven her hard. But always with love, she'd thought at the time.

Now she wondered if Dirk had done all those things for her, or for him. Maybe he'd been making her over to satisfy his own ego and pride. After all, a salesgirl in a dress shop who couldn't even read properly was not exactly a suitable wife for a brilliant lawyer.

Laura's head sank down into her hands, her head whirling. I have to stop this, she groaned inwardly, or I'll go mad. No matter what Dirk was once, he's bad news now. That's the bitter truth. The only one I can rely on.

Dusk rolled in around five-thirty, as did a very cool sea breeze, and she was finally forced to abandon her beach sanctuary. But there was no way she was going home yet. Dirk would still be waiting for her to show up.

At times like this Laura deeply regretted her lack of family and friends. If only there were some warm, welcoming home she could go to; people she could talk to. Other than Morrie and Carmel, of course.

A mental image of Hester's kind face popped into her mind.

I don't even know where she lives, Laura pondered as she walked back to her car. Or her home telephone number. I suppose I could look her up in the telephone book. There couldn't be too many H. Appleyards listed, even in a city the size of Sydney.

Laura stopped, a frown on her face. But hadn't Hester said she lived with someone? Some man? She wouldn't want me bothering her on her weekends. No...I'll just have to fill in time by myself. Have a meal in town at McDonald's then go to a movie. After that, I should be able to safely go home.

The movie was a shocker, both in content and quality. Laura would have walked out if she'd had somewhere else to go. But she hadn't, so she sat there in mutinous silence, watching some maniac murder one woman after another for God knew what reason, feeling highly irritated that she had spent good money on such rubbish.

What annoyed her most was the stupidity of the victims. Why would a woman, after being warned that there was a homicidal maniac in her suburb, deliberately walk down a dark, secluded alley by herself in the dead of night? The girl was *asking* to be murdered! Which she was, of course. Truly!

Still...even irritation could be a distracting emotion, something Laura realised when the credits finally came up and the lights came on. Not once, over the last two hours, had she thought of Dirk. A minor miracle!

But as she left the cinema she was very definitely thinking of Dirk. Surely by now he would have discarded the idea of catching up with her, wouldn't he? At least for today. It was after nine-thirty. By the time she'd walked to the car-park, made her way down to Lower Level Four where her car was, then driven through the city and across the bridge to her unit at Milson's Point it would be ten, at least.

Dirk liked to be in his office promptly at eight on a Monday morning, and had always made a habit of never having a late night on the Sunday. Laura didn't think he would have changed in that regard. Or would he? Everything else about him had changed, she accepted bitterly. She shook her head in frustration and started heading for the car park.

Laura turned into her street shortly after ten. It was a narrow thoroughfare, with not enough real room for on-street parking. Nevertheless people who didn't have garages had to park somewhere, and each night cars lined the street, perched half up on the pavement in order to give two lines of traffic enough room to pass.

As she crept down the street, Laura scanned each side for a sign of Dirk's metallic blue Jaguar. An easy car to spot, she conceded with a degree of reassurance.

It wasn't there.

She even drove past her block of units, going right to the end of the street, checking all the cars down that end.

The only Jaguar in sight was a jet-black model. Heaving a deep sigh of relief, she swung the car round and headed for her garage.

Maybe it was the sort of movie she'd just seen— or her concern over Dirk—but Laura was decidedly jittery while hurrying up the quiet and dimly lit internal stairwell. It wasn't till she was safely inside her unit that she realised she had been actually holding her breath. Once she'd slotted the security chain firmly into place, her lungs emptied in a rush.

'Silly me,' she laughed. But the laugh came out shaky and nervous.

Shivering a little, she snapped on the hall light then headed for the bathroom to run herself a bath. This was her Sunday-night ritual these days, having a long, relaxing bath last thing, usually after watching one of the movies on television. The hot water seeping into her bones was a good sleeping-tablet.

In truth, Laura had developed a whole range of evening rituals to get herself to sleep at night. Sometimes she exercised furiously. Other times she worked at her sewing like a demon till she almost fell asleep over the machine. She also kept a wide range of books beside the bed to read if sleep still eluded her. Not romances, though. She never read those any more.

If all else failed she sometimes—but not often— resorted to the tablets the doctor had prescribed for her after her mother died, and which she hadn't taken till Dirk's visit had compounded her grief with despair. For a while there she had relied on them far too heavily, but after Morrie gave her the job of making costumes for the show she had been able to wean herself off the addictive brutes by sub-stituting hard physical labour.

Laura sighed as she leant over the bath and ad-justed the temperature of the steaming water coming out of the taps. Thinking about all her little rituals made her realise how pathetically lonely her life had become. How...empty.

She straightened and stared at herself in the bathroom mirror.

'You're going to have to do something about it,' she told herself sternly. 'You're going to have to start looking for someone else to share your life with.'

Muttering some more advice to herself under her breath, she stripped off all her clothes and tossed them in the clothes basket. Her big toe told her the water was still a little hot, so she fixed that, stuffed her hair up in a shower-cap and lowered herself carefully into the bath.

'Ah,' she groaned, and leant back, the depth of the bath water pushing her body upwards till it was floating. She closed her eyes and made a valiant attempt to let her mind float in much the same way.

Futile.

It kept churning away with all sorts of self-recriminations and half-baked resolves which, by the time she climbed out of the water again, only served to tell her that life without Dirk had become meaningless, and that it would be a long, long time before she could look at another man with either trust or interest.

Reaching for one of the thick red towels that brightened up the stark white bathroom, Laura briskly rubbed herself dry, then liberally applied her favourite lavender talcum powder. The shower-cap was summarily dispensed with, sending her long dark waves tumbling down round her shoulders.

When Laura tried to run her fingers through it, she couldn't. Knots abounded from her day at the beach and long hours of not caring what she looked like.

Sighing, she picked up her hairbrush from the vanity unit and began stroking the glossy black locks back into order. Her arms were lethargic from the bath and she found the vigorous brushing a real effort. Still, if she didn't put some order into it before going to bed, God knew what it would be like in the morning.

Her gaze automatically drifted to the mirror as she stroked and she was just thinking she had caught some sun on her nose and cheeks when Dirk materialised at the edge of her reflected vision.

Shock sent a spurt of adrenalin rushing through her body. Wide-eyed and heart pumping madly, she spun round, hopeful to find that his appearance in the mirror had been a hallucination.

For a hallucination he looked breathtakingly real. Dressed casually in blue jeans and a grey sweatshirt with 'NEW YORK' written on it in bold black letters, Dirk looked even more vibrantly male than he had in his dinner suit the previous night. He was also staring at her nude body with decidedly hungry eyes.

'How...how did you get in here?' she demanded in a strangled voice, snatching up a towel and holding it in front of her nakedness.

His right hand slid into the pocket of his jeans and he pulled out a set of keys, idly twirling them on the end of his index finger.

Laura groaned. How could she have forgotten that he still had keys to this unit? Just because he'd never used them before...

'I let myself in around nine,' he drawled, replacing the keys and leaning nonchalantly against the door-jamb. 'You weren't home.'

'You mean you were in here all the time?' she gasped.

'I was sitting in the dark in the lounge, patiently waiting for you to finish your bath, waiting till you were...ready.'

She glared at him, her insides stiffening when his eyes shifted to the mirror behind her. She could actually feel his gaze travel slowly down the reflected view of her still naked back till it stopped on the swell of her bare buttocks.

'Do you mind?' she snapped, and wrapped the towel right around herself, sarong style.

His smile was both amused and sardonic. 'Such maidenly modesty. Have you forgotten I've seen it all before?'

'No,' she bit out. 'I haven't forgotten. But that was when we were living together, and when I thought you loved me! If you want to play Peeping Tom then do it with your precious Virginia.'

His smile widened, sending a prickle of apprehension quivering down her spine. 'You look incredibly desirable when your temper's up, do you know that? Your skin glows and your eyes flash. And those lovely breasts of yours lift up and down with quite tantalising movements.'

Laura tried desperately to still her excited breathing, but to no avail. Once again, she was being caught up in a turmoil of anger mixed with passion. One part of her wanted to strike out at Dirk, both verbally and physically. That other part—the one that refused to accept that this man no longer deserved either her love or desire—*it* wanted to pull him into her arms, to kiss him quite fiercely, to demand that he obliterate the past horrible year in an orgy of mad lovemaking.

Keep thinking about Virginia, she lectured herself. And all the other women he's had since he left you. Think about them whenever you start weakening.

She tossed her hair back from her shoulders, her chin tilting up, her nose going with it. 'I suppose there's no point in my asking you to just leave, is there?'

'No.'

Her teeth clenched down hard. 'I have no intention of going to bed with you,' she stated with an icy control that amazed her. If he only knew what she was thinking as she kept her eyes coldly steady upon him.

'I realise that,' he agreed lazily.

Laura tried not to look too surprised. Or disappointed. 'Then why are you here, for heaven's sake?'

He levered himself upright and bestowed an incredibly sexy smile upon her. 'To seduce you, of course.'

Now she gasped. 'But you just said...I mean——'

She broke off when he started walking slowly towards her.

'Seduction suggests an initial lack of co-operation,' he said. 'But I aim to persuade you.'

'Don't do this, Dirk,' she choked out, one hand lifting to her throat in an appallingly weak, defensive gesture.

'Don't do what?' he whispered, taking that hand and holding it first over his thudding heart, then lifting it to his mouth. 'Don't do what I know you really want me to do? You laid your cards out on the table last night, Laura. Don't try bluffing me. It won't work.' And, turning her hand over, he stunned her by taking each finger in turn into his mouth.

For several seconds, Laura couldn't think, her head swimming with the blood roaring through it. But then the import of what Dirk was actually doing rocketed her fury to much greater heights than her rapidly escalating arousal. Snatching her hand away, she went to slap him, but he grabbed it. In desperation she swung her other arm but it too was captured.

'Don't fight me, Laura,' he warned, his voice thick with desire as he ground both her arms down behind her back. 'I don't want to hurt you.'

An anguished whimper formed in her throat. Hurt her? When had he done anything else but hurt her?

'I hate you,' she sobbed, even as he drove her back against the vanity's edge and started kissing the base of her throat. 'Hate you,' she repeated, even when her head tipped back more easily to receive his ravenous lips.

'Hate me all you like,' he muttered against her swiftly heating flesh. 'As long as you let me do this...' And his mouth slid up the long, slender column of her throat finally to claim her lips.

Laura's struggle with her conscience was brief. Only later was she to puzzle over how a single kiss—however expert—could tip her so quickly into such a dark abyss of mindless submission. All she could conclude was that by then Dirk hadn't needed to do much to attain her complete surrender, having already spent considerable time attuning her both mentally and physically for this moment. Her seduction had begun over a week earlier, with the sexy looks he'd given her in the foyer of the theatre. From that moment, he had kept her mind focused singly and solely on sex every time he met her, first at the party after the show, then the following Friday night at the restaurant, capped off by his efforts last night.

But all this rationalisation was to come much later. For now, she wasn't thinking at all, her senses being swept along on a rising tide of pleasure and passion. She moaned softly under the onslaught of his lips and tongue, totally uncaring when he ripped the towel away from her body. She actually gloried in the sensation of his chest rubbing against her bare breasts, then thrilled to the possessive feel of his hands as they cupped her naked buttocks and pulled her hard into him.

Suddenly, she was spun around in his arms and held against him in front of the mirror, both their chests heaving. Her blue eyes widened when his hands started roving hotly over the front of her body, her mouth going dry as she watched her own responses to their highly erotic journeys. Her head swam in a type of dazed sensuality at his rough possession of her flesh, his hands sweeping upwards to mould her swollen breasts within his palms, lifting and pressing them together, his thumbs rubbing the sensitive peaks till they were like hard little pebbles, aching and exquisitively sensitive.

When his head bent to suck at the soft skin of her throat, a fierce spurt of desire surged through her. Her lips gasping apart, she twisted her neck round to seek and find his mouth, crying out his name in a tortured, pleading voice.

With a groan he covered her eager, open lips. And it was while he was kissing her that his hands slid down across the flat of her stomach, down between her thighs. Laura gasped away from his mouth, her back arching in reflex to his intimate invasion. Never had she felt such electric sensations, at once breathtakingly sharp yet incredibly arousing. Soon she was pressing back into him, writhing in pleasure against those tantalising, tormenting fingers.

'Oh, God,' she moaned, fearing her body was rushing headlong for an explosive release. 'Stop... please stop.'

'Never,' he growled, and with one sweeping movement she found herself up in his arms and being carried towards the bedroom.

For a split second her conscience surfaced again, but she beat it down. This was what she wanted, what she *needed*. Not all the self-lecturings in the world were going to stop her now!

But as he laid her on the bed the last shreds of her pride demanded she fight for one important concession from him.

'Dirk,' she whispered, her arms still around his neck.

'Yes?'

'You... you won't go from me to her, will you? I... I couldn't bear it...'

His momentary hesitation to answer her was like a knife in her chest, the feeling so sharp that she almost cried out with the pain. And there she'd been, pretending to herself that she didn't love him any more. Good God, hadn't she had enough evidence yet to make her realise that only love could make her act as foolishly as this? Why else would she be here now, letting him use her body, letting him break her heart all over again?

'Don't be silly, Laura,' he ground out. 'I told you. I'm finished with her. You're all I want, all I've ever really wanted.'

And as if to convince her further his mouth smothered hers in a tempestuous kiss full of such savage passion that when he temporarily deserted her to strip off his own clothes Laura was left lying there in a state of dazed delight.

'Now,' he muttered, returning to stretch out beside her, his hands stroking possessively down her quivering nakedness. 'Let's make up for lost time...'

Laura stared up at the ceiling, listening to Dirk's even breathing beside her, knowing that she too should be asleep, knowing that in a couple of hours she would have to get up and start getting ready for work. But she was far too excited to go to sleep, a strange state of affairs since her body should have been limp and sated with sexual satisfaction.

Already they'd made love several times, with Laura both surprised and stunned to find that the great sex life she'd imagined they'd once shared could actually be improved on. The answer had to lie in herself, she realised, since Dirk wasn't doing anything so differently. He'd always been a vigorous and imaginative lover. But where once he'd had to seduce, or persuade her into some of the more uninhibited foreplays and positions, now she was more than willing.

How surprised he'd been when she'd suggested they bathe together, not to mention at how comprehensively she'd washed then dried him. Of course, he had eventually turned the tables on her, enjoying her own initial astonishment, then insisted on making love to her again in front of the mirror, *really* making love this time. But any mild

shock had soon been overcome by the over-
whelming pleasure she'd experienced once Dirk had
put his demands into stunning action. Even now,
she still felt flutters in her stomach at what a wanton
picture her reflection must have presented as she
was swept to another shattering climax.

'Why aren't you sleeping?' he murmured from
the pillow beside her.

She turned her head towards him. 'I can't. I'm
too stirred up.'

'*Still*?' His laugh carried a dry amazement.

'I was thinking of us in the bathroom,' she whispered in a suddenly shy voice.

'Mmm.' He rolled over to face her in the semi-
darkness. 'Don't tell me you didn't like it.'

'Of course I did, but I think I still prefer making
love in bed. It's more . . . loving.'

Dirk made a scoffing sound. 'And ultimately
more boring. Married couples should be forbidden
to make love in bed after the first year. If they were,
marriages wouldn't run into the sexual problems
they run into. Husbands would be forced to use
their initiative, and wives would be...' He chuckled
drily. 'Well, they wouldn't know what to expect
next, would they?'

Quite abruptly, Dirk slid an arm underneath her
and pulled her over on top of him. 'I aim to keep
you in a perpetual state of expectation, my darling,'
he promised huskily. 'Expectation and arousal.'
And he pulled her down on to his mouth once more.

Laura gasped away when Dirk's lips and hands began to stir her again. 'We can't keep this up, you know,' she protested breathlessly.

'Speak for yourself. I'm doing fine.'

Which he was. She could feel that too.

'You're wicked,' she laughed shakily.

'You'd better believe it.'

'Stop that!'

'Stop what?'

'You know...'

'Oh, you mean stop doing this?' And, rolling her over, he started making love to her yet again, imprinting on her brain and her body that she was his, no matter what, for better or worse, for richer or poorer, in sickness and in health, till death them did part.

For nothing else will part us again, she vowed fiercely. Not other women or having babies or Dirk's male ego or any other stupid damned thing! He's back in my life and my bed, and I don't intend ever letting him go.

'I'm going to fall asleep at work,' she sighed afterwards.

He was still holding her close, his fingertips trickling up and down one arm. 'Take the day off,' he suggested. 'I'm not due in court today. We could sleep in, then lunch out somewhere, then go over to my place. You've never seen my bachelor pad, have you? It's right on Bondi, overlooking the beach.'

Something shrank inside herself. It was one thing to vow to put other women out of her mind. Quite another to actually do it. She couldn't bear to see where he'd taken Virginia and the others, where he probably did all the things to them he'd just done to her. There was only so much she could stand.

'No,' she said quite sharply. 'I haven't. And I don't want to.'

'Jealous, Laura?' he taunted softly.

'Yes,' she didn't mind admitting.

'Good,' he muttered.

Her temper flared right out of control, all her nobly self-sacrificing resolves obliterated in the face of his lack of sensitivity. 'Why is that good?' she bit out, propping herself up on one elbow to glare down at him. 'How would you like it if I had flaunted men in front of you? What if I told you that where you're lying now hasn't always been empty since you left me?'

Dirk jerked upright, real shock in his eyes. 'Don't play games with me, Laura,' he rapped out. 'If there's another man—or men—in your life, I want to know now! Hell, woman...' He grabbed her and pushed her flat on the bed. 'If you've been sleeping around, I'll... I'll...'

He was looming over her quite fiercely when a strange shock registered in his gaze. Laura got the impression of an unwanted realisation dawning on him. It didn't take her long to jump to the conclusion that this discovery involved his feelings for her.

Had it just come to him that he really loved her? That his feelings far transcended lust? Had the image of her being with other men finally brought the truth home?

Gathering himself, he released her and lay back down on the bed, an ironic expression on his face. 'Sorry,' he muttered. 'That was uncalled-for. I have no right to be jealous of anything you did over the past year. I guess I was just worried. After all, you were the one who wanted to know last night if I was taking silly chances. I certainly hope *you* haven't. I'd like to know so that I can take precautions in future.'

Laura lay there, trying not to look smug. You don't fool me, Dirk Thornton, she was thinking. You love me. You've always loved me. That's what this is all about. That's why, once you saw me again, you couldn't stay away.

'There have been no other men,' she stated simply. 'I was trying to make you jealous.'

His laughter was dry. 'And you succeeded. Now...' He rolled over to face her. 'Have you made up your mind what you're going to do today?'

'Yes. I'm going to go to work. I have to. The summer orders are due out this week and Hester can't do it all by herself.'

'I see,' he sighed. 'I should have known I wouldn't be able to change too many things about you. Always playing by the book, aren't you?'

'That's not such a bad thing,' she murmured, hurt by his criticism.

'And what if playing by the book doesn't work? What if you have to bend the rules a little to get what you want?'

She wasn't quite sure what he was alluding to. His job as a defence lawyer? Or his rather radical pursuit of her? 'Then you have to be prepared to take the consequences,' was her thinking reply. 'Society has a way of punishing its rule-breakers.'

Again he laughed, the cynical sound disturbing her.

'Well, that's a chance I'll just have to take.'

'What exactly are we talking about, Dirk?'

'About us, of course.'

'What about us?'

'About the relationship we're about to have.'

'Which is?'

'We're going to live together in sin.'

Now it was her turn to laugh. 'Don't be silly, Dirk. We're married, as you enjoyed reminding me recently.'

'Ah, but we won't be once our divorce goes through.'

'But . . . but I thought . . .'

'Oh, no, Laura. I told you once and I'll tell you again. Marriage is not for me. We're still getting divorced, my love. Now don't look so upset. I'm all yours, for as long as you want me. You do want me, don't you?' he added teasingly.

'Yes, of course, but——'

'No more buts, Laura. Life is for living, not worrying over inessentials. There nothing for you to worry about anyway. I'm going to be a very faithful lover.' He gathered her close. 'Now you just close your eyes and get some shut-eye, otherwise poor old Fenwick Fashions might be minus one head buyer in the morning.'

Laura might have argued with him further, if one thought hadn't overridden her startled distress at his still wanting a divorce. He loved her. He'd always loved her. That much was clear now and, no matter what he said or did, nothing was ever going to shake her belief in that again.

CHAPTER NINE

'BYE, darling,' Dirk murmured, and leant across to give her a lingering kiss. 'Do you want me to be a proper gentleman and run round to open the car door for you?'

'Don't be silly. You'll get wet.' Monday had dawned drizzly and Laura had really appreciated Dirk's driving her to work instead of her having to catch the train and walk. 'I have my trusty umbrella here.'

'You won't change your mind and call in sick?'

'I can't,' she said regretfully, pressing her hand to his lips as he went to kiss her again. 'Pick me up this afternoon?'

'Of course. I'll be here with bells on.'

She laughed. 'No bells, please. This gorgeous new car of yours will do.'

A wry smile creased her mouth. How strange life was sometimes! If she'd known the black Jag parked down the street last night had been Dirk's, she wouldn't have gone home. And she wouldn't be feeling so deliriously happy today.

Laura bestowed a loving glance on her handsome husband. 'I must go now.'

He sighed and settled back in the driver's seat. 'Cruel. That's what you are. How about lunch?' he tried again, his face brightening like an excited child's. 'I could pick you up and whisk you off to a motel somewhere, and we could——'

She was out of the car in a flash, her soft laughter hiding the rush of desire his words evoked. If she didn't get away from him fast, she would turn to mush. Whipping up her umbrella, she turned to wave a reproachful finger at him. 'I'm sure you have as much work to do today as I have. I'll see you at five and not a second before.'

She closed the door on his mock-groan, smiling as she watched him drive reluctantly off down the street.

Still smiling, she turned and immediately saw Claudia standing under her own umbrella a couple of yards away, a shocked expression on her face.

For a second Laura cringed with embarrassment—till she saw the funny side of the situation. It brought a quick smile to her face, which stunned Claudia all the more. 'Hi, Claudia,' she said chirpily. 'How was your weekend? Mine was great.'

Claudia simply gaped at her. 'But...but...wasn't that your husband in that car? I mean . . . not many men have that colour hair and . . . and . . .'

'Yes, it was Dirk,' she freely admitted, thoroughly enjoying Claudia's reaction.

'You're . . . back together again?'

'Yes, we are.'

Claudia's mouth opened then snapped shut, her lips pursing. 'I hope you know what you're doing, Laura,' she said tartly. 'I realise that your husband's a very handsome, sexy and successful man, but if I were his wife I know *I* couldn't turn a blind eye to what he's been up to lately. My God, June tells me it's been a different woman every week or so. Do you honestly think he's going to give up all that excitement and spice to settle back down with little old you? You might think you're God's gift to men but, believe me, even *you* could become boring to a man after a while.'

Laura stiffened, an angry resentment firing her tongue. 'How nice of you give me the benefit of your kind advice, Claudia,' she lashed back icily. 'Now let me give you some back in return. What I do in my private life is my business and mine alone. But let me inform you that you know *nothing* about my husband except what some silly secretary tells you and what the rumour-mongering journalists write in papers and magazines. To go out with a woman is not necessarily to sleep with her. I'll have you know that Dirk is a wonderful man. Warm and caring and sweet. Yes, sweet! Nobody knows the real man except me. If I, as his wife, choose to turn a blind eye to some indiscretions made while we were separated, then I have every right to! Because I love my husband and he loves me!'

Claudia eyed her back with openly savage hatred. 'Does he, now? Well, he has a peculiar way of showing it. Still, maybe some women like being treated like a doormat. But don't say I didn't warn you.' And with that she spun round and swept into Fenwick Fashions, leaving Laura fuming on the doorstep.

She was putting down her umbrella and muttering away to herself when Hester raced up the path and on to the step next to her.

'Trust it to rain when I left my umbrella at work,' she grumbled, brushing the rain-spots from her smart camel-coloured coat before giving Laura a swift but all-encompassing glance. 'You're looking very smart for a rainy Monday morning, Laura,' she complimented. 'Purple suits you. You should wear it more often. I haven't seen that dress before, have I?'

'I don't think so,' Laura replied rather distractedly. Her run-in with Claudia was still going round and round in her mind.

'Well, it certainly shows off your figure a bit more than the tailored clothes you usually wear,' Hester said pointedly. 'It's *very* sexy.'

Laura frowned down at her dress. It was made in soft wool, with a simple cross-over bodice, a softly flaring skirt, and long straight sleeves. It wasn't an overly clingy style, but the wide matching belt emphasised her small waist, and consequently her hips and bust. Dirk had originally bought the dress for her a couple of years previously, and when she'd been scrambling around this morning trying to find something to wear he'd reached into the wardrobe and thrown it over on to the still rumpled bed.

'Wear this,' he'd said. 'And these underneath...' A black satin corselette and bikini panties had swiftly followed. They'd been presents from

Dirk aeons ago. And it had been aeons since she'd worn them.

'I don't usually wear such sexy underwear to work,' she'd hedged.

He'd walked over and cupped her chin, his eyes glittering as they caressed her. 'Wear them for me,' he'd rasped. 'I'll enjoy thinking of you in them all day.'

Naturally, she'd been unable to resist such a seductive request.

But now, with Claudia's comment, she suddenly felt self-conscious in the dress, and what she was wearing underneath it.

'Oh, my goodness!' Hester burst out. 'I just remembered. You were going to meet Dirk on Friday night to ask him for a divorce.' She glanced sheepishly over her shoulder as several people pushed by them on their way to work. 'Sorry,' she said with a much lowered voice. 'I didn't mean to blurt that out in public, but I'm just dying to know what happened. Come on . . .' She slipped one arm through Laura's elbow. 'Let's get into the office and you can tell me all about . . .'

Laura groaned silently. She had the awfullest feeling that Hester would, in her own more tactful way, be as condemning of her actions as Claudia had been. But there was no way of getting out of telling her. On the way into the office she decided to take the plunge and tell her about Dirk's sterility as well. That way Hester would at least understand why she was doing what she was doing.

'Well, that's the long and short of it,' she finished at last. 'You probably think I'm a silly romantic fool to believe he still loves me but I do!'

Hester sat at her desk, gnawing away at her bottom lip, saying nothing. But her face told a worried story.

'OK,' Laura sighed. 'Tell me what you're thinking.'

'What I'm thinking...' Hester shifted in her chair. 'Well, I think you *might* be right about his loving you, but quite frankly I think you're still setting yourself up for disaster.'

Laura heaved a ragged sigh. 'I knew you'd say that. I just knew it. Claudia saw me getting out of Dirk's car this morning and put her views forward in no uncertain terms. She more or less told me I'm a naïve nincompoop. And she's probably right.'

'She is *not* right! You're as sensible a girl as I've ever met. If you believe Dirk loves you then he probably does. But he still can't give you a baby, Laura. Neither do I believe he'll change his mind about the divorce. From what you've told me he was a pretty wild character before he met you. You changed him for a while, but when your relationship seriously faltered he reverted to type. Loving a man like your Dirk is a great risk.'

'Why do you say that?' Laura argued. 'If my love changed him once, it can change him again.'

'Maybe. Maybe not. I haven't much faith in men changing. Frankly, I think he was perfectly honest when he said he wanted you as his mistress. He wants you all right, but only on his own selfishly male terms. If you can accept his conditions, you have a chance of some happiness with him. But it could be short-lived.'

Laura listened to all Hester said with an open mind. But, much as logic told her the woman was making a lot of sense, some inner instinct refused to accept any of it. Dirk loved her. *Really* loved her. That was her gut feeling and that was what she was going to listen to. Not Claudia, or Hester, or anyone else. It was *her* happiness at stake. As such, she had to make her own decisions.

Hester sighed. 'Yes, well, I've seen that look before. You've made up your mind, haven't you? It's do or die with Dirk, and heaven help anyone who gets in your way!'

Laura was taken aback. And showed it.

Hester laughed. 'Didn't you ever realise how unswayable you are once you've decided on a course of action?'

Laura blinked. That was what her mother had said about her when she'd got engaged to Dirk: that she was a stubborn fool and one day her pighead-edness would be the death of her.

'Don't worry,' Hester sighed. 'I'll be here to pick up the pieces.'

Laura's chin lifted. 'There won't *be* any pieces!'

Hester's smile was wry. 'See what I mean? One-eyed. But your loyalty to your husband is com-mendable. I wish *I* could be as trusting.'

The phone rang on Hester's desk, thereby ter-minating their conversation for a while. Five minutes later, Hester was on her way out of the office to inspect a shipment of clothes that had just come in from overseas.

Laura languished at her desk all morning, trying to concentrate on completing the summer orders, but not getting far. Her mind was understandably not on the job. She might have asked for Claudia's help, if it hadn't been for their altercation that morning. As it was, she struggled on by herself. By one o'clock, she'd broken the back of the job, but was at screaming-point, and was about to go for a brisk walk when there was a tap on her office door.

'Come in,' she called out, thinking ruefully that at least it wasn't Claudia. That girl didn't know how to knock.

A perfectly strange man walked in. Around fifty, with a pot-belly and a balding head, he gave Laura the once-over in silence, nodded wryly, then walked towards her desk.

'You must be Laura Thornton,' he said. 'Chap told me to give you this...' he handed over a folded note '...then to take you back to him. But be quick, honey. My taxi's parked in a no-parking zone.'

Laura opened and read the note.

'It's been four hours since I touched you,' it said. 'And I'm going mad. An hour. Just an hour. Is that too much to ask?'

She looked up at the waiting taxi-driver and tried not to blush. 'Um—where *is* this chap?'

'Outside a motel two blocks from here.'

'Oh...' Now Laura *did* blush.

'Well, are you coming or not?' the taxi-driver demanded impatiently.

Laura bent down to pick up her bag beside her chair, then stood up, her insides beginning to quiver. Never had she done anything so outrageous, so shocking!

The taxi-driver's eyebrows lifted as he looked her up and down. 'Lucky bastard,' he muttered under his breath.

Laura coloured even more fiercely. 'He...he's my husband,' she spluttered.

His glance was cynical. 'Sure, sweetheart. I make my living taking wives to their husbands at motels. Come on. Shake a leg.'

Laura was grateful it was a very short trip to the motel, and she tumbled out of the taxi on to the pavement and into her husband's arms in sixty seconds flat. While Dirk paid the driver, a quick glance assured Laura that at least the motel wasn't sleazy. In fact it was a very clean new building, with a wide glass entrance flanked by fountains and palm trees.

It was still a motel, however, and everyone knew what people booked into motels at lunchtime for.

'He thinks I'm a hooker,' she whispered to Dirk as the taxi accelerated away, her face flushing with a helpless mixture of embarrassment and excitement.

Dirk's laugh showed perfect teeth before he kissed her right there in front of everyone walking by. He'd obviously been home to shower and shave for he smelt marvellous. He looked marvellous, too, dressed in black trousers and the softest of jumpers, its steel-grey colour matching his eyes. 'Did he?'

he murmured, and, sliding a possessive arm around her waist, he led her inside. 'Well, why not?' he smiled, extracting the key of room twenty-three from his pocket. 'You've certainly hooked me...'

The whole week was like that, with Dirk constantly surprising and intriguing her. Each night after work he would take her home where she would shower and change before dressing in clothes he either chose or bought for her. They were always subtly sexy dresses made in materials that were soft to touch, and styles that flattered but never over-exposed her figure. It was her underwear that did that, highly erotic garments in either black or white that alternately covered and revealed her curves in a mixture of satin and lace.

Once she was powdered and perfumed to perfection, he would then take her out to dinner at some surburban restaurant that was attached to either a hotel or motel, so that he didn't have to drive anywhere after the meal. Laura was usually slightly tipsy by the time Dirk steered her to the pre-booked suite or room. But her intoxication was not all due to the wine she drank with her meals. She was drunk on Dirk's love and lovemaking, being almost as insatiable as he was. She couldn't get enough of his body and each night it would be many hours before they fell asleep in each other's arms.

The first hiccup in their dream existence came on the Friday evening. Dirk had rung Laura at work just before five saying he wasn't going to be able to get away from his office till seven. He had a late appointment with a client. When she offered to cook him dinner at the unit, he agreed, saying he'd be there around eight.

But eight had come and gone without Dirk.

By eight-thirty Laura was frantic with worry, yet she couldn't bring herself to try his office number. For the first time, jealousy and suspicion raised their ugly heads.

The client was a woman, she began thinking. A sexy woman. A beautiful woman. Dirk was having her right at this moment in his office. On the floor. On his desk.

Laura began to pace around the flat, her imagination going wild.

A key sounding in the front lock around eight thirty-five sent her racing to the door.

'Why didn't you ring me to say you'd be late?' she flung at him.

'I would have if I'd had a car phone,' he returned mildly, and shut the door. 'There was a hold-up on the bridge. A small collision.' His intelligent eyes raked over her tense, flushed face. 'I'm only half an hour late, Laura.'

Her jealousy was not to be denied. 'Half an hour is plenty of time for a Casanova like you! Not that that's all the time you've had. For all I know you've been at it all day. Or at least since you rang this afternoon!'

His right hand shot out to close around her wrist, yanking her hard against him. 'Don't be so bloody stupid. I was busy, as I told you. But I guess I'll just have to convince you of that, won't I?'

His mouth claimed hers with a long, savage, draining kiss. When she leant limply against him, he hoisted her high into his arms and carried her swiftly to bed.

'Hungry?' he murmured afterwards, their love-making for once having been a tempestuously short union.

'Not really.' She was lying with her head on his chest, all the storm of a while ago having been pacified.

'You're crazy, do you know that?' he said, stroking her hair, picking up the glossy black locks one by one and pressing them to his lips. 'As if I would even *look* at another woman while I have you. I love you, Laura. You must know that.'

Her head jerked upright, her lips gasping apart. 'Do you know that's the first time you've said that since... since...?'

An enormous lump filled her throat, moisture filling her eyes. Two big tears rolled over the rims and down her cheeks.

The sight of them visibly distressed him. 'Oh, God, don't cry, darling. *Please* don't cry.' And he hugged her to his heart, holding her with trembling hands. 'I *do* love you,' he insisted. 'Despite every-thing I've done. Always believe that.'

'You won't ever leave me again, will you?' she pleaded.

'No. Never.'

'And the divorce? I don't want a divorce, Dirk.
I don't want an affair. I want you here with me,
for always. Please, darling... Move back in with
me. Be my husband again.'

He sighed. 'If that's what you want.'

She lifted her head. 'Oh, Dirk...do you mean
that? Oh, I do so love you, my darling. It doesn't
matter about the baby. Truly, it doesn't. If you can't
be the father, I don't want any children. Truly.'

A grim bleakness crossed his eyes. 'I'm glad to
hear that, Laura. More glad than you perhaps
realise.'

'We...we won't talk about it any more,' she
rushed on, frightened of the subject. That was
where it had all started to go wrong before. And
what she said was quite true. She did only want
children if Dirk could be the father.

But there was one small part of her mind that
kept reminding her that fathering a child was more
than a biological action. One could be a father
without ever having impregnated the mother. One
day, in the hypothetical future, when their marriage had the security of years behind it, she might
mention this fact to Dirk.

Meanwhile, she aimed on keeping what she had
here, right in her hands.

'Perhaps we should eat now,' she suggested with
a happy sigh. 'What do you think?'

The telephone ringing startled both of them.

'Don't answer it,' he urged.

'I have to. I never get phone calls. It must be
important.'

Laura leant across Dirk's chest to pick up the receiver from the bedside table. 'Yes?'

'Thank God I've caught you at last!' Carmel exclaimed. 'I've rung every night this week and you haven't been at home. I was beginning to think you'd gone on holiday. Or is there a new man in your life?'

Dirk grabbed the phone. 'No,' he ground out. 'An *old* one!'

There was a shocked silence on the other end for a few seconds, and Laura almost giggled.

'Dirk?' Carmel eventually croaked out. 'Is that you?'

'The one and only. What did you want Laura for? She's busy at the moment.' He winked at where she was lying across his stomach, trying not to burst out into hysterical laughter.

'Oh...I...I was just going to ask her over for a barbecue tomorrow afternoon. I promised her last weekend and——'

'What time?' he cut in.

'I thought around four, but...but...'

'We'll be there. And Carmel, buy plenty of steak. I've an appetite like a horse these days.'

He put the phone down with a wide grin on his face. 'Never known that woman to be at such a loss for words. Poor Morrie. He's going to cop an earful tonight, I'll warrant.'

'Dirk, you're wicked!' Laura spluttered.

'Not as wicked as I'm going to be if you don't get that sexy tail of yours out of this bed and into the kitchen. Go on. Get going.' He rolled her over and smacked her lightly on the buttocks. 'Didn't you hear what I told Carmel? A man needs his sustenance, particularly after what I've been doing all week.'

She sat up and swung her feet over the side of the bed, pushing the thick black waves out of her face. 'A woman's work is never done,' she mocked, then stood up to walk slowly towards the door.

'Aren't you going to put some clothes on?'

The look she darted over her shoulder was very vampish indeed. 'I have an apron in the kitchen. That'll do.'

'Come to think of it,' Dirk drawled as he climbed out of bed, 'I always wanted to learn how to cook.'

CHAPTER TEN

DIRK slid his black Jaguar into the kerb and switched off the purring engine. The clock on the dashboard showed two minutes past four.

Swallowing nervously, Laura glanced up the steep path at Morrie and Carmel's house. It was one thing to laugh at her sister-in-law's stunned reaction over the phone the previous evening, quite another to face the barrage of probing questions the other woman would hit her with all afternoon.

'What do you want me to say to Carmel?' she said tautly.

Dirk shrugged. 'The truth, I suppose.'

Laura frowned. 'What exactly *is* the truth, Dirk?'

His sidewards glance was so sharp that it startled her. 'What are you saying, Laura? Have you changed your mind about wanting me back as your husband? Is that it?'

'No, of course not. But when I mentioned over breakfast that you wouldn't be needing your bachelor pad at Bondi any more you avoided answering me. If you're really serious about making a go of our marriage, then why would you want to keep paying the rent on that place?'

'I'm not paying any rent. I own it. In fact, I own the whole building.'

Laura turned to him with mouth agape. Dirk had done very well for himself over the years as a criminal defence lawyer. He would also inherit quite a lot of money when his parents passed on. The Thorntons were loaded. But Morrie's and Dirk's father did not believe in bestowing unearned wealth on his sons, deeming they had to make it on their own. So, while Dirk was comfortably off, Laura didn't think he had sufficient money to buy a block of units overlooking the beach at Bondi.

'Dirk, you haven't been getting mixed up with any unsavoury characters again, have you?'

He laughed. 'Could be, Laura. Could be. Come on, it's after four and——'

She grabbed his arm and stopped him getting out of the car. 'Oh, no, you don't, Mr Evasive. I want to know right now how you got enough money to buy that building.'

His expression was wryly amused. 'You won't like it,' he warned.

'Maybe not, but I'd still rather know.'

'OK, but don't say I didn't warn you. A few months back I represented a bookmaker in court on an assault charge. When he was acquitted he was so grateful, he gave me a couple of tips for the following Saturday's races. I put his whole fee on them in an all-up double.'

'How much was his whole fee?'

'Five thousand.'

'You bet five thousand dollars on a *double*?' she exclaimed, shocked. Dirk had always been partial to a bet on the races but he never bet more than a hundred dollars and he never, ever backed on doubles. He always said it was hard enough to pick one winner, let alone two.

'Don't have a hernia, Laura. They both won. The first at ten to one. The second at twelves. I picked up six hundred thousand dollars.'

'S-six hundred thousand,' she repeated limply.

'Yep. I put the lot in my pocket and walked straight into an auction of near-city properties and bought this nice little block of half a dozen flats. They were a bit run-down but I've been working on them myself and...'

Laura stared at him. 'You're working on them *yourself*? You, who can't hammer a nail in straight?'

'Yes, well, people change, Laura. Circumstances change them. I've quite enjoyed fixing them up, really. The only one left that's unrentable at the moment is mine. Quite frankly, it's a mess.'

Surprise held Laura silent. And there she'd been, imagining him taking women back to a sleek bachelor pad which had all sort of built-in decadent devices such as dimming lights and automatic music and revolving beds. Maybe she'd been seeing too many old Rock Hudson-Doris Day movies on late-night television.

Or maybe he'd merely taken them to motels, as he'd taken her this past week. Maybe he'd gone to *their* places. Maybe he——

Her thoughts were broken into when she saw Nicholas hurtling down the path towards them, Carmel hot on his heels.

'How many times have I told you not to run, you bad boy?' his mother yelled after him. 'You'll fall and break your neck one of these days. That is, if I don't wring it first!' She stopped halfway and stood there in exasperation with her hands on her hips, since by this time Nicholas had made it safely to the pavement and was being swept up high in his uncle's arms.

Laura had not even noticed Dirk get out of the car.

'And how are you, my adventurous lad?' Dirk laughed, swinging the boy around in a large circle before hoisting him up on his shoulders. 'Goodness, your mummy and daddy's house is still there! Haven't you burnt it down or blown it up yet?'

Nicholas giggled and wrapped his arms around his uncle's neck, holding on tight.

'Dirk, don't say things like that!' Laura rebuked as she climbed out of the car. 'He'll get ideas.'

Both uncle and nephew grinned over at her and for a split second Laura stood transfixed. They were so alike, she realised. Both good-looking devils. Both risk-takers. Both with the ability to charm if the need arose.

It immediately crossed her mind that if she and Dirk could have had a son together he would probably have looked like Nicholas—all blond curls and blue eyes and bold, effervescent energy. Her heart turned over with instant dismay and she reefed her eyes away, grateful to hide her face while she shut and locked the car door. But, even with her back to him, Laura could feel Dirk's eyes upon her, could feel his intuitive gaze boring into her back.

When she finally turned round, he was still frowning at her. Had he seen her pain? Guessed her thoughts? Dear lord, she hoped not. Thinking about his inability to father a child might give her the occasional heartache, but that was nothing to the pain she'd felt living life without him.

Putting a breezy smile on her face, she glanced up to where Carmel had been joined by her young daughter. Donna was looking quite pretty in jeans and a colourful top, her normally long, straightish hair now short and curly. It really suited her that way, disguising her thinnish face.

'And who's that gorgeous creature up there with you, Carmel?' Laura called out. 'She looks kinda familiar but I just can't——'

'It's *me* Aunty Laura!' Donna burst out. 'I've had my hair cut and look . . . it's all gone curly, like Nicholas's.'

Nicholas made a very male scoffing sound. 'I hate curly hair,' he muttered. 'I want *straight* hair, like Uncle Dirk's.'

'It'll get straighter as you get older,' Dirk assured him. 'It's in your genes.'

The little boy cocked his head on one side and frowned down at his uncle. 'But I don't have any jeans.'

Dirk and Laura looked at each other and laughed.

'Come on, you two laughing love-birds,' Carmel reprimanded with a dry edge to her voice. 'We have a barbecue to get ready and a lot of questions to be answered.'

'Are we going to play Trivial Pursuit, Mummy?' Donna asked innocently.

'I don't think so, darling. I think your Uncle Dirk and Aunty Laura have played enough games lately.' And, throwing them both a drily reproachful glance, she turned her daughter by the shoulders and ushered her back up the path.

Dirk grimaced. 'Get ready for the third degree,' he whispered low under his breath as they began making their way slowly up the path, Nicholas still riding on Dirk's shoulders.

'You're the defence lawyer,' she hissed back. 'Tell me what to say!'

'How about . . . I refuse to answer on the grounds that it might incriminate me?'

'Very funny. I don't think Carmel's going to swallow that.'

'Then just tell her I came to you and told you I was sorry for the way I'd acted, that I still loved you and wanted you back. She's a typical woman. Mention the word "love" and they invariably melt.'

Laura's heart and step faltered for a moment. For wasn't that exactly what he'd done? And hadn't she melted, like the typical woman he'd just spoken of rather disparagingly?

Don't start thinking like that, a panicky voice warned her. You have to trust him. If you don't, your relationship is doomed.

'What's the matter?' Dirk asked, stopping to look back from where he was now, a few steps ahead of her. 'Have you forgotten something?'

'Yes, I—er—just realised we didn't bring any wine or anything.'

'Don't let that worry you. Morrie's cellar is going to outlast Morrie. Come on, this chap weighs a ton. What have you been eating, Nicholas? Ninja Turtles?'

The boy burst forth with a gleeful peal of laughter. 'You're silly, Uncle Dirk. You don't eat turtles.'

'Haven't you heard of turtle soup?' he asked as he lowered Nicholas on to the front porch.

'No... Is it nice?'

'When you come over to visit Aunty Laura and myself, we'll let you try some. There's also kangaroo-tail soup and alligator steaks and——'

'Come on, Uncle Dirk,' Donna wailed from the doorway. 'Daddy's waiting for you to help. You know he always burns the steak if you don't keep an eye on him. Mummy says he shouldn't drink and cook at the same time.'

'Neither he should.' He turned to slide a warmly possessive arm around Laura, urging her into the house.

Dirk was right about Carmel. She readily accepted the simple 'love' explanation of how their reconciliation came about. She was also tactful enough not to bring up Dirk's womanising, although she did drop the occasional clichéd excuses such as 'boys will be boys', and 'no use crying over spilt milk', and 'love cures everything' and 'life wasn't meant to be easy'.

Personally, Laura thought life could never be easy—and that love was not the universal panacea people thought it was. She loved Dirk and she still believed he loved her. But was love going to be enough?

All afternoon, she couldn't stop looking at him and thinking about what Hester had said: that she was setting herself up for disaster with him. Why her faith in him was suddenly being shaken she couldn't fathom.

Perhaps it's because he's changed, she finally decided. Before, during the first years of their marriage, he'd been so open with her, telling her all about his work, his feelings, his life. He'd held back nothing. They'd shared everything. Now, he seemed to want to compartmentalise his life. There was his work, his innermost feelings and ambitions. And then there was his sex life.

Once, she'd been an integral part of the whole. Now she was relegated to the last part only.

Female intuition told her this change in her husband had undoubtedly been caused by the discovery of his sterility—as had his burst of mad woman-chasing. He'd not indulged in that kind of activity till he'd found out the unfortunate truth. Still...if she wanted to remain Dirk's wife, she had to accept there was no going back, and he would never be the same person she'd first married.

What worried Laura most, however, was whether she could keep on loving a man who could only express his love for her one way. In bed. Her mother's experience and repeated warnings to Laura as she grew up had ingrained in her a deep distrust of men who were like that—where love was a shallow, one-dimensional emotion, little more than lust. And lust didn't last.

'Something's worrying you,' Dirk stated casually once Morrie and Carmel abandoned them to see to their children's baths.

Laura was sitting in one of the comfy family-room armchairs, sipping a glass of red wine. Dirk was leaning back on the sofa, doing likewise.

She glanced over at him. 'Why do you say that?'

'Come now, Laura. I know you through and through. You're usually fairly talkative when you've had a drink or two. Today, you've been exceptionally quiet. On top of that I couldn't count the times I caught you frowning at me. I began to think my fly was open.'

Laura resisted the urge to laugh. Both she and Dirk were wearing jeans and sweaters, but Dirk's were so old and faded and tight that if his fly had been open it would hardly have passed unnoticed by all and sundry.

'Come on,' he probed. 'What's bothering you?'

Dared she say anything? Much as she was concerned about the future, she had to admit that the past week had been the most exciting, sexually satisfying week of her life. It was as if they were on their honeymoon again.

A light went on in her brain.

Of course! Goodness, why was she so stupid? It *was* as if they were on their honeymoon. After their long separation it was only natural that sex would be at the forefront of their relationship. Given time, it would naturally calm down to a more normal rate. Meanwhile, what did it matter how often Dirk wanted to make love to her? Or where? Or when? Or how? Or even that he preferred sex to talking? Most men would be the same. Heavens, they had all the time in the world for long and meaningful discussions. She would be crazy to waste her husband's inordinate passion for her. Literally crazy!

'Laura,' Dirk said warningly, 'if you don't say something in the next couple of seconds, I think I'm going to explode.'

The smile she sent him was more than seductive. It was downright wicked. 'Let's go for a drive somewhere, Dirk,' she whispered huskily. 'Somewhere private...'

His eyes widened, but he was quick enough to put his wine down and stand up. 'You'll have to drive. I'd be over the limit. You should be all right, though. That's only your second glass.'

'So it is.' She lowered the crystal goblet on to the side-table and stood up, aware that a quivering had already started inside her.

Still, Laura was astonished by the storm of sensation that swamped her when Dirk slid his arms around her to cup her tightly jeaned bottom. He drew her hard against the outline of his arousal, taking her mouth in a kiss that sent her head spinning into outer orbit.

Carmel came back into the room while they were kissing, clearing her throat quite loudly.

When Dirk finally pulled back, Laura swayed on unsteady legs. He held her tightly against his side to keep her knees from buckling and shot his sister-in-law a rueful look. 'I hope you don't mind, Carmel, but Laura and I have to leave. Right away.'

Carmel's understanding smile was a testimony to her love for them both. 'No worry. Morrie won't mind either. He's ecstatic to see you both together again. Anyone would have thought he'd had a hand in it, the way he was carrying on upstairs.'

Dirk's fingertips dug almost cruelly into Laura's hip as he urged her abruptly forward.

'Say goodbye to the kids for us, will you?' he asked of Carmel. 'And tell Morrie I'll give him a call very soon. Oh, and thanks for the food. The steak was great and the salad delicious. I feel revitalised.'

Carmel walked with them to the front door. 'I'm not so sure that's a good thing. Laura here is looking a mite peaky. Why don't you two try sleeping at night for a change?' she suggested drily.

They left her waving to them from the door, a knowing smile on her face.

'I don't think you realise how strong you are,' Laura complained, once they were making their way down the path in single file and his iron grip had left her flesh. She rubbed at her hip. 'I'll have bruises in the morning.'

'They wouldn't be the first I've given you lately,' he teased.

She swung round and punched him playfully in his stomach. 'Beast!' Then she hit him again, with both hands, rather enjoying the feel of her fists striking the hard wall of flesh.

'I'll have bruises!' he squawked in mock pain.

'You'll have more than bruises by the time I've finished with you tonight.'

His eyes widened. 'I'm intrigued. What will I have besides bruises?'

'Terminal exhaustion,' she quipped, and, whirling back round, dashed ahead of him down the path.

'I'm getting fed up with you coming into this office every Monday morning all bright-eyed and bushy-tailed,' Hester moaned a fortnight later. 'People in love should be quarantined so that other poor sods don't have to suffer witnessing such disgusting happiness.'

Laura laughed. 'Had a bad weekend, did we? Have you finally kicked out that less-than-perfect male specimen you told me you're living with? What's his name, by the way? Nigel? Bruce?'

Hester pulled a face. 'Do you think I'd live with a man named Nigel? Or Bruce? Heaven forbid! My boyfriend happens to have a very nice masculine name, and, if I tell you, you must promise not to mention it to anyone. Especially anyone around here.'

She sounded so mysterious that Laura's curiosity was aroused. 'Do tell.'

'His name is Drake. Drake Marshall.'

'Drake Marshall? Oh, my God, you don't mean *the* Drake Marshall, do you? The resident hunk of *Our Street*?'

'The same,' Hester said smugly.

Laura's eyes narrowed when she saw Hester grin widely then wave her left hand over the top of her desk. One would have to have been almost blind not to spot the huge rock sparkling on her ring finger.

Laura jumped to her feet and ran over to inspect it. 'Why, you sneaky rat!' she exclaimed. 'You've been having a love-affair with every woman's dream man and you didn't breathe a word. When did he ask you to marry him? This weekend?'

'He's been asking me for months. But I wanted to be sure, his being an actor and all. They're not exactly renowned for their faithfulness.'

'Do you really love him? I mean ... it's not just the fame and fortune, is it?'

A warm glow came into Hester's rather cool beauty that Laura had never seen before. 'I'd die for him.'

'Oh, Hester,' Laura groaned. 'That's the most romantic thing I've ever heard.'

Both women looked at each other, tears shimmering in their eyes.

'I've never been so happy,' Hester choked out. 'I'm almost afraid it can't last.'

'I feel that way sometimes,' Laura agreed, thinking of how ecstatically happy she'd been with Dirk this last month. 'But you can't live life thinking like that. Nothing comes with guarantees. All you can do is give it your best shot. Whatever happens, happens.'

'You're a grand girl, Laura,' Hester said sincerely. 'You deserve the best life can bring. I sure hope that husband of yours knows what sort of wife he has in you. Not many women would be as understanding. Or forgiving.'

'Oh, I don't know,' Laura laughed shakily. 'I'm not that forgiving. If I ever caught him with another woman, I don't know what I'd do.'

CHAPTER ELEVEN

'SOMETHING wrong, Dirk?' Laura said within seconds of his arriving home that evening.

He spun round from where he was pouring himself a stiff Scotch at the bar in the living-room. 'Why do you ask?'

'It isn't like you to drink during the week. Fridays, yes. And the weekend. But never on a Monday.'

His smile was wry. 'Am I that readable?'

'Not even remotely.' She smiled as she came forward to lay both her hands on his chest, looking up at him with love in her eyes. 'But I know you pretty well. I'm also getting better at reading your body language.'

'Mmm. That sounds promising.'

When he went to kiss her, she pulled back, dismayed that his only way of communicating with her these days was through sex. They had finally settled down to a more normal lifestyle, staying in for dinner most nights, but Dirk's desire for her had not flagged in any way. And while Laura adored being made love to so beautifully every evening, there were times—like now—when she just wanted to talk.

'Please, Dirk, I want you to talk to me, not kiss me.'

'You're beginning to sound like a wife,' he reproached with a dry laugh, and turned away to pick up his Scotch.

'Maybe that's because I *am* your wife,' she returned with hurt in her voice and worry in her heart. What kind of marriage was this if her husband couldn't—or wouldn't—share his troubles with her? Certainly not the sort of marriage that could possibly last.

'You're treating me like a mistress again, Dirk,' she went on worriedly. 'I...I don't like it.'

He turned back to stare at her before slowly lifting the whisky glass to his lips. His gaze was steely over the rim, his expression implacable. And yes...annoyingly unreadable. Only one thing was certain in Laura's mind. He wasn't going to tell her a thing about what was troubling him. Not a single thing.

'Don't you really love me, Dirk?' Laura asked, her voice catching.

A dark cloud passed over his eyes, turning them to slate. It was a colour they always went when he was furious, or when an opposing lawyer backed him into a corner from which he couldn't emerge a clear winner. 'Of course I do,' he ground out, and drained the glass.

Did she believe him? Oh, dear God, if he was only using her again she would just die!

'Laura...' The frustration in his eyes melted as his gaze swept over her stricken face. 'Don't torture yourself so. Of course I love you. Haven't I told you so a hundred times these past weeks? What more can I say or do?'

She shook her head, her eyes dropping to the carpet, confusion in her heart. For she wasn't sure if Dirk's idea of love was the same as hers.

'I shouldn't have moved back in with you so quickly,' he muttered. 'It was a mistake.'

Her eyes flew to his, panic in her heart. 'No, it wasn't. It *wasn't*!' And she flung her arms around him, hugging him tightly. 'Don't say things like that, Dirk. You make me afraid that you'll leave me again, and I couldn't bear that.'

He sighed, his arms enfolding her, his own hug a more gentle, restrained gesture. 'I would never do that. Never...' He set her away from him, his smile warm and tender and infinitely reassuring. 'Now! What say we have some of that delicious food I can smell simmering away in the oven, and then we'll have a game of Scrabble?'

Laura's heart leapt. Scrabble had been one of the ways Dirk had helped her with her reading. The bold black print on the large square-set letters had seemed to fix words in her brain more easily than from a page in a book. She had admired his patience in playing game after game with her, knowing it must have bored him to death. But he'd never looked bored. Still, the only way they'd been able to make the game even remotely competitive was for her to have a start. Even then, he'd always won.

'I'll give you fifty start,' he offered.

'Only fifty! Make it a hundred and you're on. Winner washes up.'

'All right. Hey!' he shouted after her as she retreated swiftly into the kitchen. 'You got that wrong, didn't you? The *loser* should do the washing-up.'

She grinned back over her shoulder. 'Nope. You should have listened more carefully, Mr Smartypants. If you win, you get to wash up. Of course...you could always throw the game and then I'd win—for the first time, I might add!'

'Methinks I have the odds stacked against me,' he grumbled.

'Methinks you have!'

It was a great evening, mainly because sex wasn't the basis of their enjoyment. They opened a bottle of wine over dinner, then afterwards played not one, but three games of Scrabble. With a start of one hundred, Laura won the first easily. In truth, her vocabulary had improved greatly since they'd last played, as had her confidence in herself. She had never enjoyed washing-up so much in all her life.

For the second game, her start was reduced to fifty. Dirk, for once, had really concentrated. But she'd still won, catching him with the 'z' unused at the end.

'I'll fix you next time,' he scowled, turning all the letters over in readiness for another game. 'No more starts, you little cheat.'

'Cheat? I never cheat.'

'Then how come you've got so damned clever all of a sudden?'

'I've been doing crosswords,' she confessed. 'Marvellous source of small, sneaky words.'

'I'll say! Now play, you dirty rat.'

'Ooh, you sounded just like James Cagney.'

'James who?'

'You don't know?' she mocked. 'And there I've been all these years, thinking you were a superbrain. I'm beginning to think your intelligence is very selective, Dirk Thornton.'

'And I'm beginning to think you're a con-artist. I'll bet you always could read properly, couldn't you?'

'Maybe,' she teased, then put all her seven letters down on the first go, scoring a fifty-point bonus. Dirk stared down at the board for a few seconds, then settled his handsome face into a determined expression. Laura resisted laughing. She had seen that look before, when she'd first refused to marry him.

He won. But only marginally.

When they had finally gone to bed, Dirk had still made love to her, but it had been altogether different, a softer, slower, more tender coming-together, such as she'd never known with him. She'd drifted off to sleep feeling content and very, very loved.

'I have to go to Brisbane for a couple of days,' Dirk informed her over dinner the following evening. 'I've booked a seat on the afternoon plane tomorrow, returning late Friday evening, or maybe

Saturday morning. I'll ring you and let you know which.'

Laura looked up, waiting for him to say more, but he merely forked some more apricot chicken into his mouth, washing it down with a swallow of mineral water.

Her disappointment was acute. So they were back to that, were they? And there she'd been after last night, thinking everything was going to be fine between them. But nothing had really changed, had it? He still wasn't going to treat her like a real wife.

'Don't you think I deserve more details than that?' she said, unable to keep the edge out of her voice. 'There was a time when you used to tell me everything about your work. Or isn't it *work* taking you to Brisbane?' she finished sharply.

Laura wished she hadn't made that last inflammatory statement as soon as she saw Dirk's reaction. His whole body stiffened, his grey eyes darkening. For a few seconds, he said nothing, then a lengthy, frustrated sigh reverberated from his lips.

'Of course it's work. What else? Quite frankly, Laura, that last little barb of yours is the very reason I didn't want to tell you too much. But, since you're so suspicious, I will, and to hell with the consequences! The fact is that I'm going to Brisbane to represent a client who's suing a company for breach of contract. When I add that that client is a woman—a very attractive woman—you might see why I didn't want to tell you.'

The muscles in his jawline were working overtime. 'I can appreciate why you might be quick to distrust me. But truly, darling,' he assured her, reaching across the corner of the table to cover her hand with his, 'those mad days of mine are over. You're all I need and want in a woman. I adore you. Do you think I'd do anything to risk losing you?'

He lifted her hand to his lips, kissing each fingertip with exquisite tenderness. 'I want to be doing this,' he said softly, 'when we're seventy years old. Even eighty.'

It was no use. Laura could not hold out against Dirk when he did and said loving things like that. What woman could?

'You'll come back Friday night?' she asked in a thickened tone.

His eyes caressed hers. 'Even if I have to fly the plane myself...'

'I don't believe it!' Hester exclaimed as she marched back into the office and plonked down in her swivel chair, pursing her lips and folding her arms. Laura looked up in surprise and trepidation. She had never seen Hester look so livid.

And then the penny dropped.

'Don't tell me,' Laura groaned. 'The order came in from Aus Evening Wear and none of the dresses are a patch on the samples the rep showed us.'

Hester blinked her astonishment. 'How did you know?'

'I didn't like to say at the time, but I wouldn't have trusted that Doug Turner as far as I could throw him. Those chauvinistic pig types are all the same. They think that if women in business are good-looking then they're nothing but empty-headed bimbos who've slept their way into their jobs and only have to be flattered a little to agree to anything. Remember how smarmy he was and how he kept saying you'd look great in his dresses?'

Hester grimaced. 'Only too well. Do you know that they've used not only inferior material but inferior workmanship as well? The finish is atrocious! God, I'm so mad, I could spit!' She glowered down at the telephone, then picked up her address book, stabbing the pages over with the point of a Biro. 'Bimbos, eh? I'll show him bimbo!' She snatched up the receiver and dialled.

Laura's heart began to pound. Confrontations tended to make her very nervous, even second-hand ones.

'I'd like to speak to Doug Turner,' Hester rapped out sharply. 'This is Hester Appleyard from Fenwick Fashions... Thank you...' She tapped the desk with the Biro in her right hand. Laura's heart jumped when Hester suddenly sucked in a sharp breath.

'I don't care if Mr Turner's in a meeting,' she launched forth, ice in her voice. 'This is an emergency, so I suggest you call him to the phone this instant or your company just might have a lawsuit on its hands!'

Laura could only admire the woman. She wasn't sure if she'd have had the nerve to be so assertive. It crossed her mind then and there that if and when she ever started up a fashion agency of her own she would ask Hester to be her partner.

'Mr Turner?' Hester resumed shortly. 'Hester Appleyard from Fenwick Fashions. Are you aware that the order of evening dresses your company has just delivered to us is of a far inferior quality to the samples you showed us earlier in the year? You're not? How surprising! Nevertheless, you personally guaranteed that they would be *exact* replicas of the samples!'

She sucked in some more air, then plunged on. 'Well, let me assure you right here and now that they are appalling. Let me also assure you that this is what is going to happen as of this moment. I'm going to stop payment on those dresses and send them back to you pronto, the cost of which will be billed to your company. We offer quality clothes to the public at Fenwick Fashions and wouldn't dream of stocking those pathetic excuses for exclusive evening gowns you had the hide to send. Please don't bother to call on us again!'

With that, she slammed the phone down.

Laura was shaking her head in admiration. 'Phew! I had no idea you could be so forceful. Does Drake know what he's letting himself in for, marrying a potential tycoon?'

Hester heaved a ragged sigh. Laura noticed her hands were still shaking. 'Probably not. He knows I've got a temper, though. I threw his dinner at him the other night.'

'You did? Goodness! What happened?'

Hester's expression became wry. 'He ducked and it hit the wall. Guess who had to clean it up in the end? But it was worth it!' Her smug smile of satisfaction showed Laura another side of her normally cool co-worker. Hester was a closet rebel.

'So!' She sat up straight and threw Laura a speculative glance. 'How are things going with you and Dirk, by the way? You looked a bit down in the mouth this morning. Did you have a little tiff about something?'

'No. But he's got to go to Brisbane this afternoon on business for a couple of days. I'm going to miss him terribly. Fact is . . . I'm missing him already. I wish I could see him off at the airport but the plane goes around three.'

'Why don't you take a long lunch? Or, better still, take the afternoon off. I'll cover for you.'

The feeling of depression that had been hovering over Laura all day immediately lifted. 'Would you? Oh, that would be marvellous. I know he's in his office at Broadway at the moment, and that's not far away—a five-minute taxi ride.'

Hester glanced at her watch. 'It's almost lunchtime now. Why don't you call up a cab and just go?'

Laura was already putting on her jacket. 'You're a life-saver, do you know that?'

'We girls should stick together,' Hester said quite seriously. 'I'll call the taxi for you while you go freshen up. Can't have lover-boy seeing you with a shiny nose and messy hair.'

Less than fifteen minutes later, Laura was paying off the cab driver outside the two-storeyed building on Broadway that housed Dirk's legal practice.

As Laura spun round to walk across the pavement and into the building Dirk's secretary emerged, busily talking to another woman. She didn't see Laura standing there and hurried off down the street before Laura could say hello.

Shrugging, Laura made her way inside and up the stairs on the left of the small lobby, half relieved that June was out to lunch. She didn't like the woman, her infernal gossiping to Claudia having caused her no end of personal anguish.

The first impending sign of disaster was the perfume that hit Laura's nose the very second she opened the door to go into Dirk's small reception area. It stopped her calling out to him, as would have been natural. In fact, she was standing there for a moment in stunned confusion, trying to recall where she'd smelt that perfume before, when Dirk's voice floated crystal-clear through the gap in the half-opened door.

'What on earth are you doing in there, Virginia? How long does it take to freshen up and comb your hair? If you don't watch it, we'll still be here when our plane takes off.'

Laura froze, her thoughts whirling. *Virginia*? *Our* plane?

'You're always hurrying me,' a sultry female voice announced after the sound of a door opening and shutting. 'So! What do you think? Will I do?'

'You always look stunning, Virginia. Stop fishing for compliments.'

'And you're always a bastard, Dirk Thornton. Tell me, what story did you feed that poor little wife of yours *this* time?'

Laura's heart stopped.

'The truth, actually,' came Dirk's chilling reply.

'Not the *whole* truth, I'll bet,' the woman scoffed. 'Truly, Dirk, what kind of cruel game are you playing with that woman? I saw her face that night at the theatre, you know. She's crazy about you. Much as I adore you, darling, I can't help feeling a little guilty, no matter what you say. She seems so...sweet.'

'She *is* sweet.'

'Then why, Dirk? Why deliberately do things to hurt her? It doesn't make sense.'

'It does to me.'

'Oh, I do so *hate* it when you go all secretive and mysterious on me! Surely I deserve some sort of an explanation. After all, we go back a long long way. You can trust me.'

He laughed. 'But I already *have* trusted you, Virginia. And I'm still trusting you.'

'Hmph! That's all I'm going to get out of you, is it? Typical! Well, I sincerely hope you've booked us into a decent hotel, you bad man. I can't stand anything but the best.'

'So I've gathered. I got the bill the other day for that little black number you bought. Couldn't you have been a touch less—er—extravagant?'

'Well, you said something extra sexy. Extra sexy only comes at a price.'

'So I've found out,' came his dry reply. 'All ready to go now? I thought we'd have a bite to eat somewhere then catch a cab to the airport.'

'Sounds good to me. Mmm, you look deliciously handsome in grey, do you know that?'

Laura lurched back out into the hallway, her legs almost going from under her. She felt sick. No, not just sick. *Shattered*.

Everything was disintegrating inside her. Any second she was going to collapse, really collapse. But some last desperate instinct told her she couldn't. Not here. Not in front of Dirk, and that horrid woman.

Dashing for the stairs, she made it out into the street where at that moment a bus was pulling in at the corner not far away. Running, she jumped on to it, not looking back.

'Where to, lady?' the bus driver said, holding out his hand for the fare.

'Anywhere,' came her dazed reply.

He sighed. 'That'll be a dollar fifty, then. We terminate at Circular Quay.'

She found two dollars in her purse, took the fifty cents change and slumped down into the nearest seat.

I'm going to go mad, she kept saying to herself, all the while fighting the nausea that was swirling in her stomach.

But she didn't go mad.

Madness, like life, was not that easy.

CHAPTER TWELVE

LAURA'S doctor gave her a certificate for a week off
work. He obligingly wrote that she was suffering
from a virus, even though both of them knew
emotional stress was the problem. He asked Laura
if she needed special help, or a prescription to calm
her down, but she declined, knowing the only one
who could ultimately help her was herself.

She made it home to the unit where, trying not
to look at Dirk's clothes hanging next to hers in
the wardrobe, she packed a small case and immediately left again. She didn't know what she was
going to do exactly, but she knew she couldn't bear
to see Dirk for a while, couldn't bear to talk to him
on the phone and pretend she didn't know Virginia
was in the hotel room with him. Neither could she
bear to confront him with the truth and hear some
more smooth lies in return.

For she didn't doubt he would lie. Lying had apparently become a way of life with him.

Was it revenge he was after? she wondered
wretchedly, as she moved her car into the line of
traffic heading north on the Pacific Highway. Or
was he just plain wicked, thinking he could have
her and Virginia at the same time, and God knew
how many other women in the future who took his
fancy?

She shook her head and gripped the steering-wheel, anguish and anger fighting for supremacy within her. What a fool she had been to have him back into her life so quickly. What a naïve, silly little fool!

Never again, she vowed with bitterness in her heart. She would rather be alone for the rest of her life than open herself up to this sort of hurt again.

She drove on north on to the expressway, over the Hawkesbury River and up into the ranges, by-passing Gosford then heading for Newcastle. She looked neither left or right, simply straight ahead, the local scenery meaning nothing to her. Her mind kept picturing Dirk coming home from Brisbane on the Friday, puzzled probably that he hadn't been able to reach her on the phone, and finding her note, which said simply, 'Going away for a while. Have to think. Laura.'

The note was not for his peace of mind. She didn't give a damn if he rotted in hell. But she didn't want him calling the police to search for her. She needed time and peace to work out what she was going to do with her life without Dirk.

She made it as far as Taree that night. And that was where she stayed, in a motel by the Manning river. A lovely spot, actually, with soft green lawns and leafy trees to walk under and just think.

For three days she walked and thought.

On the fourth day, she collapsed. Just slid off a chair in the motel dining-room on to the pink-carpeted floor, waking some time later to subdued voices hovering over her, lying on her bed in her room. She was dimly aware of people leaving the room and a strange man sitting down on the side of the bed and picking up her wrist to check her pulse.

'Mrs Thornton? I'm Dr Jenkins. The motel manager called me. He said you were a visitor from Sydney and wouldn't know any local doctors. How are you feeling now? Better?'

The room gradually stopped swimming. 'Yes,' she whispered. 'I . . . suppose so.'

'Have you been ill lately, Mrs Thornton? The manager seemed to think you might have been, and you do look pale.'

'In a way . . .'

'Would you like to tell me about it? Maybe I can help you.'

Her smile was wan. 'I don't think so.'

The doctor sighed. 'Young women like yourself shouldn't faint for no reason. Have you fainted before, Mrs Thornton, especially of late?'

She frowned and shook her head. 'I've never fainted in my life.'

'Ah.' The doctor nodded slowly. 'Then could it be, Mrs Thornton, that you are pregnant?'

Her stomach fluttered, her eyes widening before the fleeting hope died and she turned her head to one side on the pillow. 'No,' she said flatly. 'No, that's impossible, I . . . I . . .'

Impossible or not, her mind automatically checked dates and she realised for the first time that her period *was* late, by a week. Against all logic, her stomach turned over. But once again common sense prevailed. 'You don't understand...' Sighing, she turned back to face the doctor. 'I *can't* be pregnant. My husband's sterile. He...he...'

Suddenly, her eyes filled with tears. She blinked furiously but two large drops had already escaped to run down her cheeks.

The doctor was sympathetic. 'Maybe your husband isn't the father of the child,' he suggested gently. 'Is that it? Is that your problem, my dear?'

'No,' she choked out. 'It's just stress, I tell you. I can't possibly be pregnant.'

'Maybe not, but I think you'd better have a pregnancy test to prove things one way or the other, just for my benefit. Then I'll feel more confident looking for other reasons for your fainting spell.'

Laura dashed away the drying tears with the back of her hand and gave another weary sigh. 'If you insist...'

The test came back positive.

'But...but that can't be!' she exclaimed, shock overriding any joy she might normally have felt at such a discovery. She was sitting on the side of the bed, wringing her hands. 'I don't believe it. I...I want another test done. A different one.'

'You'll have to come back to my surgery for that,' the doctor frowned.

'I don't mind. I *have* to make sure.'

The second test, too, came back positive. *Very* positive, the doctor assured her. As did the third she insisted upon the following day.

Gradually, Laura's shock became almost anger.

'But how can this have happened?' she demanded of the doctor, going on to explain that her husband definitely believed himself sterile, and that this belief had changed him radically, had virtually wrecked her marriage, ruined her life!

The doctor was unable to give her any real answers other than a mistake must have been made. Maybe the pathologist got the tests mixed up, or maybe her husband's sterility had been a temporary thing, caused by some problem other than a past case of mumps. There were many factors that could cause a drop in sperm count, he said. Some medications, heavy drinking and smoking, excessive physical training, even too much sex could do it on occasions!

'But Dirk didn't have a drop in sperm count,' she said impatiently. 'He had no sperm count *at all*!'

It was while Laura was arguing over the whys and wherefores of Dirk's sterility that the reality of her pregnancy finally sank in. A mistake *had* to have been made, she eventually accepted—a monumental mistake!

She sat there in the doctor's surgery, silent and stupefied. And then it hit her again. She was going to be a mother. She was going to have a child. Not any man's child, either. *Dirk's* child.

Laura burst into tears.

The doctor handed her tissues and patted her on the shoulder. 'There, there, Mrs Thornton. Think of it as God's miracle to heal the rift between you and your husband. He'll want his child, won't he?'

Laura's heart contracted as she once again heard her mother saying that men like Dirk didn't really want children. She also heard Dirk's own voice confessing the same. But then came a vivid picture of Dirk laughing and hoisting Nicholas up on to his shoulders and she just *knew* he'd been lying about that. He *did* want a child. She was sure of it!

Laura really had no option. She had to go back home and tell Dirk about the baby. After that, it was up to him what part he wanted to play in his child's life. She wouldn't stop him having access, but as far as she was concerned their marriage was still over. Irretrievably and irrevocably over.

Wiping her nose, she stood up. So did the doctor, his face worried.

'You won't do anything...silly, will you, Mrs Thornton?'

Now it was her turn to do the reassuring. 'Of course not, Doctor. I want my baby. And I'm sure my husband will too, once he really thinks about it. Thank you for all your help and kindness.'

'Wait, I'll write you out a prescription for some iron tablets. And make sure you see your doctor as soon as you get home; will you do that? Frankly, I'm not keen on your driving all the way back to Sydney by yourself. Couldn't you catch a train? Or fly?'

'I'd rather drive. And truly, I feel fine now. I'll look after myself, don't you worry. I won't let anything happen to me or my precious baby.'

The doctor smiled then. What a lovely young woman, he thought. And what a fine mother she was going to make. God, some men were such bloody fools!

It was late Monday afternoon by the time Laura reached North Sydney, right in the middle of peak-hour traffic. She eased her car off the main road into the side-street that led to her place, her stomach in knots at the thought of confronting Dirk and telling him he wasn't sterile after all.

Time had eradicated her conviction that he would welcome this news. She'd been wrong before about Dirk. She could easily be wrong again.

The sight of his new black Jaguar parked in one of the twin garages allotted to their unit confirmed his presence inside. Dirk didn't catch trains or buses or even taxis. He drove everywhere. If his car was in, so was he.

Leaving her luggage in the boot, Laura made her way reluctantly up the stairs and along to her door. She'd slipped the key in the lock and was in the act of turning it when the door was reefed open before her. Dirk was standing there, looking as ghastly as she had ever seen him: eyes bloodshot, his hair a shambles, and a three-day growth on his chin.

'Laura!' he rasped. 'Thank God. I've been worried sick!' And, grabbing her, he pulled her inside, kicking the door shut behind her.

When he tried to hold her, she pushed him away. 'Don't touch me, Dirk,' she bit out.

Those red, bleary eyes searched her face, anguish in his expression when she eyed him back with a chilly reproach. 'You know, don't you?' he groaned. 'About Virginia...'

She didn't bother to admit or deny it. 'How could you, Dirk?' she said in a low, pained voice. 'How *could* you?'

He groaned and leant back against the wall, raking unsteady hands through his hair. 'Hell,' was all he said.

Her blue eyes might have seemed cold as they looked him up and down. But her swift scrutiny of his half-naked body left her feeling far from cold.

Considering all he had done, Laura found this incredible vulnerability of hers quite sickening. There he was, dishevelled and hung-over, dressed in nothing but a pair of decrepit jeans. And she still wanted him.

Not only wanted him. *Loved* him.

She had to be quite mad.

Laura shook her head, wondering what she was going to do to survive this situation. Perhaps she should turn round and leave again, go away somewhere and never tell him about the baby.

No...

She couldn't do that to him. He had a right to know, no matter what the outcome.

'I don't want to discuss you and Virginia, Dirk,' she began brokenly. 'But I have something to——'

'*No!*' he cried out, with such torment in his voice and face that Laura was stunned into silence. 'No!' he repeated, and grasped her hands, squeezing them tight. 'I know what happened on Tuesday. I rang Hester and was able to put two and two together. I know what you thought you saw and heard, Laura. But you're wrong. Dead wrong. I...I...'

His hesitation snapped Laura out of it. This was what she'd feared—that he would try to con her again, that he would *succeed*!

'No more lies, Dirk!' she screamed back at him, wrenching her hands away. 'I can't bear any more lies!'

'Neither can I,' he groaned back. 'Dear God, neither can I. But you must listen to me, Laura. You must give me a chance to explain why I did what I did. For pity's sake, just give me five minutes of your time before you condemn me. Is that too much to ask, measured against a lifetime? Five miserable minutes?'

Oh, he was good, she thought bitterly. He was very good. And she was too weary to fight him. Too spent.

'All right, Dirk,' she sighed. 'Five minutes. But I...I think I'd better sit down,' she added when the room suddenly spun around her.

'Are you all right?' Dirk asked, worry in his voice as he led her into the lounge and settled her on the three-seater.

She swallowed then lifted her chin, eyeing his apparent concern with cynicism. 'I'm fine, thank you. Just say what you have to say, Dirk. And please keep standing. I don't want you near me.'

He reeled from her words as though she'd struck him. 'Morrie warned me about this,' he muttered under his breath. 'But I wouldn't listen. I was too stubborn, too sure of myself, too bloody stupid!'

'You've wasted almost a minute,' she reminded him icily.

He threw up his hands and paced across the room, whirling round at the far wall to almost glare over at her. 'I won't have you shut me up,' he ground out, grey eyes blazing. 'I will have my say no matter how long it takes. There's too much at stake here, Laura, to indulge such things as imaginary hurts and female pride.'

Laura stared over at him, and thought how magnificent he looked, standing there, fists clenched, bare chest puffed out, shoulders squared. The ultimate male animal, cornered but never beaten, coming out fighting till the death. Such a male animal in the wild would always become the master of the pack, she realised. He would be the stallion to which all the mares came for mating; the ram who serviced a whole flock of ewes; the stag on the crest of the mountain whose antlers were bigger and stronger than all the rest.

No wonder I fell in love with him, she conceded bleakly. No wonder...

He took a couple of steps towards her, his defiance melting to a look of such anguish that Laura was thrown. This was not the Dirk she'd just seen. Where was his arrogance now? His ego? Certainly not in the bleak eyes that were raking hers.

'I don't know where to start,' he confessed shakily, and rubbed the sides of his face in a most uncharacteristic gesture of uncertainty. 'God, why didn't I see this as a possible outcome? Why didn't I see what I was risking?' His hands raked through his hair again, his voice becoming as agitated as his actions. 'I'm not doing this at all well, am I?' His bark of laughter was dry and hard. 'Remind me never to defend anyone close to me in court. I'll make a hash of it.'

Laura could only sit there and stare at him. Never had she seen him like this. Never!

A faint crazy hope wormed its way into her heart that maybe all *wasn't* as it seemed. This was a real, heart-rending emotion she was seeing here. This was true distress. Maybe there was some miracle explanation that would make things come out right after all. Only *what*?

'You asked for no more lies, Laura,' he said tautly. 'Fair enough. No more lies it is...'

He began a controlled pace up and down the room, talking all the while, his words both astonishing and incredible.

'I told you once I didn't love you when I married you... That was lie number one. Of course I loved you. I loved you so much, I would have killed for you! I loved you then, I loved you when I left you, and I love you now!'

Laura's whole breathing ceased. Dear God, don't let this be another lie, she prayed.

'Lie number two... I said I preferred living a carefree bachelor life to marriage and a family.' His laughter was bitter now. 'Hell, I *hated* being alone, hated being without you. Why do you think I put all that money on those stupid horses? Because I didn't care. I thought you didn't love me any more. I thought—oh, who gives a stuff what I thought then? I was wrong. I knew that the moment I saw you after your mother's funeral. The way you looked at me, Laura—it tore my heart apart. I wanted to take you in my arms right then and tell you how much I loved you. But something held me back, some germ of an idea that had been running around at the back of my mind for quite a while...'

He scooped in a deep, steadying breath. 'Which brings me to lie number three... My sterility...'

Laura's heart leapt back into life. It thudded away in her chest, hardly daring to anticipate what Dirk was about to say. Oh, the madness of the man if it were true. The crazy, wonderful madness!

'I was watching television one night,' he went on, 'when a programme came on about infertility in couples. There was a whole segment on women who couldn't conceive because of psychological problems...'

Dirk stopped pacing then, sending a pleading glance Laura's way. 'I don't think you ever realised just how warped your mother was about men, how deeply her twisted ideas had been planted in your subconscious. Oh, yes, on the surface, you thought you trusted my love for you; but underneath, Laura, lurked a fear that my love was only lust. The only thing that would soothe that fear *was* my giving you a baby, because in your eyes—and your mother's—a baby born in wedlock was the only true test of a man's love. The trouble was, your mother had also made sure you didn't really believe such a love existed. Your underlying lack of faith in my love was stopping you from becoming pregnant, Laura. At least . . . that was what I'd concluded.'

Laura opened her mouth to deny this, then shut it again. Maybe he was right . . . Who could be sure about the complex workings of the human mind?

Dirk expelled a ragged sigh. 'That conclusion began to dominate my thinking. So I set about finding a way to give you the baby you so desperately wanted. I didn't care what I had to do to achieve that end. I became convinced that if I could somehow separate sex and love in your mind you might conceive. My plan was to invent a scenario where you would let me make love to you, but where falling pregnant was the last thing you would think of. Which is why I told you I was sterile, and why I made you think I was a heartless Don Juan who only wanted a woman for one thing.'

Laura licked very dry lips. 'You mean you . . . you didn't really sleep with all those women, didn't say and do all the things with them you did with me?'

Dirk groaned, moving quickly to fall to his knees in front of her, grasping her hands to his. 'I never touched any of them. Not a one. They were all ex-clients, or friends of ex-clients who went out with me a couple of times as a favour. They weren't women who cared much if people gossiped. People had been gossiping about most of them all their lives. Hell, I spent a fortune on ritzy restaurants and nightclubs getting myself a reputation as a ladies' man, believe me!'

'You didn't sleep with *any* of them?' Laura repeated dazedly. 'Not even Virginia?'

'Certainly not!' Dirk levered himself up off his knees and sat down beside Laura, peering deep into her eyes. 'How could I when I was so in love with you? Why do you think I almost panicked when you started making love to me that night at Morrie's? I hadn't been with you in nearly a year and suddenly there you were, the woman I loved, going to do what you were going to do. I felt my body racing away to imminent disaster and I had to get out of there as fast I could. I said the first thing that came into my mind. Oh, I know I hurt you abominably, saying what I did, and I could have bitten out my tongue later. But all I could think of was getting out of there before I made a complete fool of myself.'

'But...but I heard Virginia say you both went back a long way. Were you lovers once?'

'No. We went to university together, and were both very involved in the university theatre group. But it was Morrie she was sleeping with back then, not me.'

'Morrie?' Laura gasped.

'My holier-than-thou brother was not always a good family man, or a saint. He certainly wasn't above using his position as chief casting director to his advantage,' he said drily. 'Virginia wasn't much better. She wanted to be an actress and she knew what side her bread was buttered on. She was also a damned interesting person, and we became firm friends, enjoying the same sense of dry wit and humour. But we never fancied each other sexually. She was too conniving for my taste, and I was not easily manipulated enough for hers.

'Over the years I've done quite a bit of contract work for her, and when she had some trouble recently she came to me again, and right away I knew she was just the sort of female I needed to make you sinfully jealous. Virginia thought I was crazy and cruel, especially when I insisted on buying her a very sexy dress for the occasion. When she objected I simply blackmailed her into agreeing by saying I wouldn't represent her if she didn't. I had completely lost my conscience, my whole mind focused on making you hate me and want me at the same time.'

'I think you succeeded,' Laura said huskily. 'For a while, at least.'

'I don't think I did,' he denied, surprising her. 'Your love for me shone through all the time, Laura, and soon I simply wanted to wallow in it. I began to hate the lie I was living. I wanted you back—not as a mistress or a lover, but as my wife. As soon as I could, I abandoned my original plan and moved in with you, clinging to the hope that your believing I was sterile would be enough.'

'Oh, Dirk...'

'Yes, yes, I know it all sounds crazy now. And cruel. Virginia and Morrie were right about that. But I honestly thought I was being cruel to be kind. I kept remembering what you said to me about how if I couldn't give you a baby you didn't want me any more. I really believed that, Laura. That's why

I left in the first place; why I put my mad plan into action. I thought giving you a baby was the only way to resurrect and keep your love. Yet strangely enough, once we got back together this time, as each day went by, I knew that you loved me for myself, and that we'd be all right even without a child. You've grown as a person, Laura. And so have I. Our love will survive, my darling, baby or no baby. You must believe that...'

'I do,' she said sincerely.

His whole face lit up with the realisation that somewhere along the line he had achieved the seemingly unachievable. Laura believed in him again. Her love was intact and everything was going to be all right.

'Oh, Laura...my dearest love...'

She took his face in her hands and kissed him. 'You are crazy, do you know that? What if I'd ended up hating you instead of being just jealous?'

'But you didn't!'

'You are an incorrigible gambler, Dirk Thornton.'

His eyes narrowed. 'Kiss me again,' he husked. She did.

'Dirk,' she murmured against his lips, her heart pounding with excitement at what she was about to say.

'Mmm?'

'I still have something to tell you.' It was impossible to keep the smile out of her voice.

Every muscle in his face froze. He pulled back slowly, a wide-eyed wonder growing in his gaze. 'Laura...you don't mean——?'

She nodded. 'Yes...your plan worked. You're going to be a father. That's what I came back to tell you.'

His mouth fell open.

'Aren't you going to say something?' she asked softly.

She watched his throat gulp several times, watched him battle with the sudden brimming in his eyes.

'It's all right, my darling,' she whispered, a lump in her own throat as she gathered him to her heart. 'You don't have to say a thing. Not a single, solitary thing.'

HARLEQUIN PRESENTS®

We've reached fever pitch!

Don't miss the climax of our sizzling selection of stories...

They're

Coming next month:

Final Surrender by Elizabeth Oldfield
Harlequin Presents #1747

Sorcha had a fight on her hands. She'd inherited fifty-one
percent of her stepfather's business—and Rui de Bragance
had been left the other forty-nine percent! It was going to be
a battle of wills, and Rui's secret weapon was sheer male
magnetism! He was gorgeous, sensual...but also ruthless
and powerful. Sorcha was out of her depth, but she was
determined never to surrender....

Available in June wherever Harlequin books are sold.

MILLION DOLLAR SWEEPSTAKES (III)

No purchase necessary. To enter, follow the directions published. Method of entry may vary. For eligibility, entries must be received no later than March 31, 1996. No liability is assumed for printing errors, lost, late or misdirected entries. Odds of winning are determined by the number of eligible entries distributed and received. Prizewinners will be determined no later than June 30, 1996.

Sweepstakes open to residents of the U.S. (except Puerto Rico), Canada, Europe and Taiwan who are 18 years of age or older. All applicable laws and regulations apply. Sweepstakes offer void wherever prohibited by law. Values of all prizes are in U.S. currency. This sweepstakes is presented by Torstar Corp., its subsidiaries and affiliates, in conjunction with book, merchandise and/or product offerings. For a copy of the Official Rules send a self-addressed, stamped envelope (WA residents need not affix return postage) to: MILLION DOLLAR SWEEPSTAKES (III) Rules, P.O. Box 4573, Blair, NE 68009, USA.

EXTRA BONUS PRIZE DRAWING

No purchase necessary. The Extra Bonus Prize will be awarded in a random drawing to be conducted no later than 5/30/96 from among all entries received. To qualify, entries must be received by 3/31/96 and comply with published directions. Drawing open to residents of the U.S. (except Puerto Rico), Canada, Europe and Taiwan who are 18 years of age or older. All applicable laws and regulations apply; offer void wherever prohibited by law. Odds of winning are dependent upon number of eligible entries received. Prize is valued in U.S. currency. The offer is presented by Torstar Corp., its subsidiaries and affiliates in conjunction with book, merchandise and/or product offering. For a copy of the Official Rules governing this sweepstakes, send a self-addressed, stamped envelope (WA residents need not affix return postage) to: Extra Bonus Prize Drawing Rules, P.O. Box 4590, Blair, NE 68009, USA.

SWP-H595

HARLEQUIN®

PRESENTS Plus

"I remember you, Annie. I remember everything...."
Mysterious phone calls were almost expected in Annie's
life as an internationally loved pop star—but there was
something different about this particular caller...
different, and yet familiar. Little did she suspect who it
was. Little did she realize she was about to be drawn into
a situation beyond her wildest dreams!

It had been a simple misunderstanding, but somehow
Benedict Savage was convinced that Vanessa had
deliberately set out to seduce him! The idea was
outrageous. Not only was he her boss, he was a
formidable sexual predator into the bargain—and
Vanessa had no intention of falling prey to his
dark charm!

Presents Plus—a passion for romance!

Coming next month:

Dying for You by Charlotte Lamb
Harlequin Presents Plus #1743
and

Savage Courtship by Susan Napier
Harlequin Presents Plus #1744
Harlequin Presents Plus
The best has just gotten better!

Available in June wherever Harlequin books are sold.

PPLUS25

Announcing
the New Pages & Privileges™ Program
from Harlequin® and Silhouette®

Get All This FREE
With Just One Proof-of-Purchase!

- **FREE Travel Service** with the guaranteed lowest available airfares plus 5% cash back on every ticket

- **FREE Hotel Discounts** of up to 60% off at leading hotels in the U.S., Canada and Europe

- **FREE $25 Travel Voucher** to use on any ticket on any airline booked through our Travel Service

- **FREE Insider Tips Letter** full of fascinating information and hot sneak previews of upcoming books

- **FREE Mystery Gift** (if you enroll before May 31/95)

And there are more great gifts and benefits to come!
Enroll today and become Privileged!

(see insert for details)

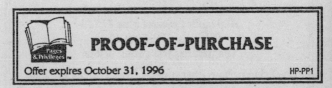

PROOF-OF-PURCHASE

Offer expires October 31, 1996   HP-PP1